ÆTHELGIFU

First Saxon Abbess

THE FIRST LADIES OF SHAFTESBURY ABBEY
VOLUME I

DEBORAH M JONES

CONTENTS

NAMES OF THE MAIN CHARACTERS

Those in CAPITALS refer to real historical people, the others are pure fiction.

KING ALFRED – the Great, King of Wessex and founder of Shaftesbury Abbey

LADY EALHSWITH — his wife and mother of his children

EDWARD, the Atheling — their older son, the presumed heir

ÆTHELGIFU — (Ath-el-ye-vu) their second daughter, Abbess of Shaftesbury

BISHOP WULFSIGE of Sherborne — whose See contains Shaftesbury

ASSER — a scholarly Welsh monk, Latin tutor and biographer of King Alfred.

GRIMBALD — a scholarly Frankish monk, building supervisor

ABBOT JOHN — of Athelney Abbey. He was known as the Old Saxon

Pepin — a Frankish monk of Athelney, a nasty piece of work

Mark — another Frankish monk of Athelney, not quite so bad

Master Chad — reeve of Shaftesbury Abbey, an important royal appointment

Alwyn — his older teenaged son, a pleasant youth

Edwin — his younger son, another decent teenager

Cynehelm — thegn of Shaftesbury burh, a rough, tough warrior of high rank

Beornwulf — an attractive Mercian lord and Abbey visitor

Matteo — a replacement for Asser as Head Latin Tutor at Shaftesbury

Wilfric — the mass-priest with a growing family

Leonfranc of Donheued — a thief.

Tild — a free Saxon youngster, servant of Æthelgifu

Skadi — a Danish slave-girl, about 13

The "Handmaids of the Lord" (also beginning to be known as Nuns):

Abbess Mildritha — of Wimborne Abbey

Edith — formerly of Wimborne, now Prioress of Shaftesbury

Clotilda — Prioress of Wimborne, after Edith

Fritha — formerly of Wimborne, now a good nun of Shaftesbury

Hild — an unhappy postulant, about 13

Wynflad — who runs the new learning-house

Gifu — popular young mistress of postulants and oblates

Tatswith, "Tate" — the foolish young Mistress of Guests

Elswith — a stern but fair Novice Mistress

Wulfthrith — the unpopular Sub Prioress, formerly of Wimborne

CHAPTER 1

LATE FEBRUARY AD 888

LEAVING

"BRING SOME WINE for Sister Æthelgifu — and a stool. Quickly now!"

The news just announced to the young nun made her momentarily giddy, swaying, the blood draining from her normally rosy cheeks. She felt the stool placed behind her legs and sat down on it, back bowed and deep blue eyes staring down unseeing at the grey stone slabs of the chapter house floor. It had never felt so cold. The faint light allowed through the small high windows, filled with bluish-green glass, fell on the dour older woman seated in an ornate wooden chair on a plinth before her.

While fighting to calm the maelstrom of thoughts swirling in her head, Æthelgifu took the proffered goblet and took sips of the rich honeyed Frankish wine. Her hand was shaking, causing the liquid to make little waves within the vessel. The servant woman took back the empty vessel and noiselessly withdrew into the shadows.

Abbess Mildritha, seated at a higher position, and with a back rigidly upright despite arthritic twinges, viewed the girl with barely contained disdain. It had taken Mother Mildritha years of religious obedience, serving in many of the offices required to progress to the present highest one: infirmarian, cellarer, novice-mistress, subprioress, prioress. Now she was acknowledged as the distinguished ruler of a dual abbey, where even the monks, in their separate quarters, obeyed her orders. She was proud that she could inspire awe and a little fear in those under her governance.

After all, she assured herself, did not her predecessors include great holy women, missionaries, who had gone with Saint Boniface to the heathen German tribes. These sainted women were reknowned throughout Christendom for their convincing preaching skills and the great number of pagans they had converted. Kings and men of high office had sought the advice of abbesses, spiritual mothers — their influence and power had been the equal of any royal or of any man in holy orders.

Mildritha was proudly aware that until the Danes destroyed so many Christian centres in the past century, the Saxon religious leaders of monasteries, both women and men, had been the drivers of culture and learning throughout the land, from Northumbria to the South. Her own abbey here at Wimborne had withstood the threat of depredations from the heathens and was still a beacon of light. Had it not been chosen out of all others in Wessex to house the bones of King Aethelred, one of the brothers of the present monarch, Alfred — and to raise royal children, such as this Æthelgifu, Alfred's second daughter? She had been placed in the care of Mildritha and the Lord's Handmaids here from the age of six as a sickly child oblate. Her health had greatly improved, she had received a good education, as her father had insisted, and she had recently been professed as a Handmaid, a nun, at her own volition. Now this, this child, a mere assistant infirmarian, given one of the lowest ranks in the community as befits her age, was to be an abbess herself.

Instant elevation.

"When you are installed in your new position, you must not neglect devotion to our great saint, Cuthburga, founder of this abbey of Wimborne and sister to King Ine and of your own ancestor, Ingild. Promise me that!"

Æthelgifu felt the cold pale-blue eyes of her Superior upon her bowed head. She shrank into her simple woollen habit, nodding obediently, squeaking "Yes, Mother", and wishing herself tiny enough to hide beneath the stool. How can this be? She tried to calm her mind to understand the enormity of what was being asked of her. "How can I, at barely sixteen, act in the way of a great abbess?" She thought. "I am not worthy, not experienced enough, not commanding enough. Dear Blessed Mary and all the saints, oh and Saint Cuthburga...help me!"

On the following day Wimborne Abbey saw the departure of Prioress Edith and three of the Obedientes, leading figures in the women's community — middle aged, capable women — sent ahead to prepare the newly constructed abbey at Shaftesbury for its first abbess. The four noble ladies, all nuns of long standing, accepted this rupture from their settled existence with holy resignation and sadness. They knew only that where they were going was newly built and that they were to be pioneers. Their new abbess was to be that young royal child they had but recently scolded for any misdemeanour. How she would govern them was known only to God.

At least they were to be accompanied by an escort of strong warriors, hand picked for this duty, as they journeyed to their new home through woods and fields, along tracks and river beds. At any time a Danish raiding gang could ambush them and hack them to pieces. Despite the king's great victory over the Vikings at Edington almost a decade earlier, rogue Danes in groups still infested the woods, especially near rivers up which they would silently row under cover of darkness. Monasteries and merchants were always their targets for rich pickings.

"Fear not, Sisters," Abbess Mildritha exhorted them. Fervent prayers and their company of armed and trained soldiers from Alfred's burh (fortified town) at Shaftesbury, would provide protection. Filled with fluctuating feelings of panic and hope, they set off on a cold day in early spring, seated with their belongings in two sturdy carts, with warriors both at the head of the procession and taking up the rear.

Several other women, from novices to aged vowesses, and from among the fully professed Handmaids to trusted lay servants, would leave Wimborne later with the abbess-to-be, to form the kernel of the new community. They were persuaded to leave behind their comfortable and secure home with the offer that they could return to their Mother House if they really wanted to. They would need only their new abbess's permission. Some would find the challenge exciting, others a penance — for the pioneering spirit is not given to everyone.

A week later, at first light and just after the Office of Laud, when the Sisters had filed into their northern cloister from the church while the Brothers of the abbey withdrew into their southern one, there arrived at Wimborne Abbey another party of armed men on horseback. These dozen soldiers were somewhat hung-over from feasting at their overnight lodging at the thegn Askell's nearby mead hall, but stirred themselves into wakefulness as they entered the abbey precinct. Edward, Æthelgifu's brother (older by a year), the Atheling, led them. This was the royal prince who would be king one day, if he proved himself and the Witan so elected.

The Handmaids, gathered in their cloister, were shielded by sturdy stone walls from the sight of the warriors, but the men's horses' hooves clattering on the cobbles, and the loud male voices, shouting and laughing, could be enticingly heard from within. Excitement spread. Great things were to happen. A quarter of the female community at Wimborne, four of the fully professed Handmaids, two novices and three vowed widows, were scurrying round, helped by their sisters and servants, preparing themselves to leave the sanctuary of the abbey to go on this great adventure with their prospective abbess. A few were in tears, comforted by their friends — some of whom were genuinely sorry to lose their companionship, others fighting back their envy. Others were flustered, running back to the dormitory to collect an item they had forgotten, or to the infirmary to collect a potion or bundle of herbs that may prove to be of use.

Those chosen to go on this mission had already packed their few spare clothes, footware and personal effects, and servants now took the bundles to four covered carts, two borrowed from friendly neighbours, which would transport the luggage and the older women. As Prioress Edith had already left a few days before, now the subprioress, the Lady Clotilda, a haughty Frankish princess, had been promoted in her place and was taking charge. She ordered the various items to be assembled which would be necessary for the new community at Shaftesbury — some pots and jars of preserved food, sacks of beets, parsnips, dried beans and peas, onions and leeks, several big rounds of hard cheese, skins of wine and drinking water, two barrels of ale, some fresh loaves, and several blankets and baskets of dried herbs. The rest of whatever food was needed would be bought from the neighbouring burh until their own lands produced sufficient, either home-grown or tithe-provided.

Having taken the vow of stability, for the rest of their lives to remain in the religious house they had entered, these individuals were now to travel, to go beyond their abbey to a far-off unseen place. There was a natural apprehension about the journey.

One young woman would whisper her concerns to another. She in turn would relate hers to a friendly older Handmaid. The serving-maids would confide theirs to each other. But none would dare voice aloud her fears, or she could be accused of lacking faith in God. Abbess Mildritha reminded them of their valiant foremothers — the saints who had ventured intrepidly into pagan lands.

Would they be safe, even with an armed escort? Not only was there danger from heathen Danish robbers, but what if a pack of hungry wolves were to attack? Even more concerning, what would they find at journey's end — fine stone buildings or humble wooden shacks? Would the provisions there be sufficient and would there be enough land to sustain them? Would the armed men, part of King Alfred's new standing army, living so close in the next-door burh, be a danger to them and to their chastity, or would they constitute a valuable and blessed defence? At least they would be welcomed by Prioress Edith and the other familiar faces.

As Abbess Mildritha clapped her hands as the signal, the chosen women emerged from their cloister into the main yard of the abbey enclosure, looking around in awe and excitement at the mounted and helmeted warriors, young men from some of the best families in Wessex, clad in leathers and furs with swords, seaxes and axes at their belts and round shields slung behind them. They in turn smiled at the younger nuns, and whispered lewd comments between themselves, laughing and insincerely apologising amid sniggers. Servants hurried in their tasks, placing all the luggage in the carts, while large strong horses were led from their stables to be harnessed between the shafts. With special care the new prioress, Clotilda, saw that a number of prepared parchment skins, and the few precious books that Wimborne could spare, had been wrapped in protective cloths and placed in decorated wooden book-hoards, and were now hidden behind the more mundane luggage. The large sack that contained woolwaste to make up into pads for the women's hygiene was placed deliberately to obscure sight of the precious literary treasures.

Then, when all the goods had been stowed, as the Handmaids and servants mounted their riding horses and the older women were installed in the carts, the Abbess Mildritha bestowed an icy kiss upon the cheek of Æthelgifu. The future Abbess of Shaftesbury then stepped up the mounting block and straddled her horse. Mildritha proclaimed a special blessing upon the departing company for a safe journey, and the party set off.

Edward took the lead with six of his warriors, then came the Handmaids, novices and servants on horseback. Those who had not ridden for years, and those who had been child oblates, like Æthelgifu, and the servants who had been too poor to ride, found that it took awhile to balance comfortably on their horses' backs and to relax into their motion.

After them trundled the carts with the older vowesses as passengers being jolted with every dip and ridge in the roadway. Occasional shrieks were heard when a cart bumped over particularly uneven ground. Two trusted slaves from Wimborne Abbey sat at the front of each cart handling the reins and goading the carthorses. The other six soldiers took up the rearguard.

The remaining community watched them leave, regretful, a little resentful, but zealously praying for their safety. Abbess Mildritha stood apart, looking grave, and wondering how her own life might have been different if she herself had been the daughter of a king and not just of an ealdorman, however close to royal status.

Through winding lanes and woodland paths frozen hard with overnight frosts of early spring, the little procession made its way through Wessex. Early dawn mists gave way to brighter skies, and some sunshine even gently warmed their backs as they travelled north. Heavy dews of melted frosts showered them with great globs of cold water as they passed under budding boughs.

Twice the sight of wolves peering around trees in the woods caused short delays while all fell silent the better to hear if more of the creatures were around. At one time a family of wild boar scampered across their track, and Edward had to forbid his warriors from pursuing them, as valuable time would be lost.

"Let the goddess Frey keep her sacred boars intact, and then maybe she will bestow fertility upon the fields. After all, my sister's abbey will need all of the harvest produce it can get!" Edward called to his men, who laughed, yet those with emblems of boars' heads upon their helmets touched them out of respect for the powerful goddess of the Old Religion.

Sometimes the wheels of the heaviest carts became stuck in the muddy ruts of the road, as the ground warmed and turned to slush. When all of one cart's wheels were particularly wedged in deep mire as they forded a brook, sinking steadily, it took six of the soldiers and four of the slaves, dismounted, to heave the vehicle onto firmer ground.

After a few hours, with the sun higher in the sky, the party stopped at a clear running stream. There both humans and horses were granted a rest and a drink, refreshing themselves with the cold clear water. The women groaned, laughing, at the ache in their hips from the hours spent straddled on horseback. They staggered round, legs apart, until their muscles adjusted. Only young Hild, a postulant just weeks away from her former life spent riding around her father's estate, could smirk at the discomfort of her elders.

Æthelgifu signalled to Edward to go deeper with her into the surrounding woods, taking the opportunity to speak alone together. They embraced warmly, and Edward laughed to see the tears on his sister's cheeks.

"It's been so long, hasn't it, since we last met? I would hardly have recognised you from the sickly little child sent away to the Handmaids at Wimborne as an oblate. What were you, six? You were a sickly child, they tell me. I honestly didn't think I'd ever see you again!"

"Oh Edward, I've so missed you all — mother and father, Athelflad and you. The other two were just babies when I left."

"And now, Athelweard is trying to grow a beard and look like a hard man! And since the age of five little Alfthryth has been betrothed to the grandson of the Holy Roman Emperor. I've not seen him myself, Baldwin the Second of Flanders. Poor girl — he's a hot-headed idiot, and a lot older than she is, but is a useful ally, apparently. His mother Judith, Charlemagne's great-granddaughter, had married our grandfather, you remember, when she was very young."

"And then she wed his brother Aethelbald as soon as grandfather was dead!"

"Yes, but they had no children. Her third husband was Baldwin of Flanders, and they did have children."

"Oh how complicated! So, did our sister know this son of theirs, Baldwin?"

"She and he met once, and detested each other on sight!"

"Oh poor little thing!" She broke off to remember the small girl with unruly blond curly hair and a ready laugh. She won't be laughing much now, she thought. Then, hiding her sadness with a wry smile, turned back to her brother. "Do you remember our lives as children?"

"Good God, yes — we were shit-scared that time we all had to escape from Chippenham, when Guthrum and his horde of Danes were about to attack it."

"And having to hide in the Somerset marshes, gathering reeds to burn, and only running about on dry higher ground when it was safe to do so!"

"And pretending to fight with sticks and having to be very quiet while father and the ealdormen of the Witan were discussing serious things we didn't understand."

"And how Athelflad learned to wield a seax and

taught us to form a shield wall against pretended Danes! And now, you're a warrior yourself, carrying a great axe and a sword!" She broke off to laugh good naturedly at the thought of her brother being a warrior. He smiled too, with a touch of pride. She then paused, and with furrowed brow, asked, "And just who are these men you're leading?"

"Well, while you were saying your prayers, Father was gathering a standing army."

"What is wrong with the system of noble thegns mustering men, the 'fyrds'?"

"That took time and, frankly, half of the peasants would sooner be ploughing or herding than fighting. So he realised that he needed to train and equip a proper army. Every community of ten households, every tithing, is obliged to send men, one for every five hides, to be trained and stand ready for any new invasion. My men are an elite part of that army."

"Are they from the Shaftesbury fortified town, I believe it's called a 'burh'?"

"These aren't from there. They are garrisoned at Winchester. There are seven hundred men based at Shaftesbury. Others are defending a series of burhs across Wessex, a day's march apart. Y'know father also had ships specially built that could overtake and destroy the ones the invading Danes use. He's a genius, our father!" They both sighed, thinking of the powerful and wise man they both loved and admired.

Edward broke their momentary contemplation, "I know Guthrum apparently converted to Christianity, but you can never trust these Danes."

"Really?" exclaimed the young religious woman, innocent of such matters.

"Sure! Their conversions could be subterfuges and anyway, not all of them are Christians. They could attack any time, anywhere. This, little sister, is why you need to trust me and my men," he said, smiling.

"Hey, less of the little! You're only a year older than I am. And what's this scar?" she reached up to his handsome tanned face and gently touched a small scar over his right cheek-bone.

"Oh, that was from training last year. Our little brother swung his sword a bit too wildly and clipped me there. You should have seen his face when he drew blood! Father was not best pleased. He made young Athelweard join him in his own Latin lessons. Y'know Brother Asser is teaching father Latin? But Athelweard, I'm afraid, is neither a warrior nor a scholar. Oh well, he's still young."

Aethelgifu smiled, then furrowed her brow again, "It must be exciting leading these warriors, but dangerous too. Do take care, Edward, and don't do anything reckless, promise me?"

"Oh stop sounding like mother!" he said, placing a hand on his sister's shoulder and giving it a gentle squeeze. "Anyway, we must get back on the road if we're to reach Fontmell Magna by nightfall."

"Oh!" Her face fell with disappointment, "We're not going to Shaftesbury tonight?"

Edward smiled. "You don't know Shaftesbury! The approach to it means we have to climb really steep hills, and descend to deep valleys, for a number of miles. Far better first thing in the morning than after a twenty mile ride. We'll be well rested and you'll arrive ready to take on all your new duties."

At the thought of all that that implied, Æthelgifu's stomach tightened into a knot and she trembled for a moment. "At least, I'm not abbess until I've been installed", she muttered to console herself, "and God may then send me the gifts I need".

CHAPTER 2
ARRIVING

EDWARD WAS NOT WRONG. The last few miles up and down, but mostly up, the hills to Shaftesbury were exhausting. The horses patiently trudged, sweating hard and billowing clouds of breath into the cold morning air. On the steeper inclines the older women walked behind the carts to reduce the weight on them, and most of the mounted soldiers also went on foot to save their horses from over-exhaustion.

Their overnight lodging had been in the hamlet of Fontmell Magna, the women huddled on wooden trestle-boards around the fire pit in the modest Great Hall, snatching sleep when their excitement allowed, chattering and giggling with nerves at other times. Æthelgifu was not in a position to hush them as she felt as giddy as they did. None of them had slept away from Wimborne since they had entered religious life there. Such novelty caused hearts to beat faster.

As she lay there, eyes open in the dark, hearing the gentle snores of those who had managed to sleep, Æthelgifu understood the meaning of the word *uhtceare*, lying awake before dawn with worrying thoughts. She realised when she had taken her final vows that this was to be her chosen life, but sometimes hoped that her father would absolve her of her vows in order to marry her to an impossibly handsome foreign prince. Her dreams were no less romantic than those of any other teenager. Once an abbess, there would definitely be no turning back.

When such imaginary longings disturbed her, she would force herself to remember all the young, some very young, pregnant women she had attended as assistant Infirmarian in the abbey hospital. She recalled their screams in childbirth, especially if the baby was not positioned easily. She suffered the loss of their babies with them, all too often. Sometimes the children would grow and be loved, then become sickly and die before the eyes of their parents, causing them terrible grief. And then so many young mothers lost their own lives, no matter how caring the nursing of them had been.

No, all that would be spared her.

While ordinary free Saxon women were not forced to marry against their will, such freedom was not permitted a royal princess. No crude warrior of her father's choosing, even a Frankish prince, would ever force himself upon her, breathing drunken fumes and stinking of sweat, claiming his right as her husband. No, better a life devoted to God than to a brute. As most noble men were brought up to fight, kill and maim, such qualities that were valued among them were not necessarily those that became a gently-loving spouse. Better a secure life filled with culture and comfort than the precarious one of a warrior's wife. So, purged of romantic temptations by realistically considering the plight of so many other women, she managed a light slumber.

The men had billeted themselves in the humble homes of the villagers, and all ate well and slept soundly. The peasants themselves, huddled in blankets around the embers of their fire pits, felt too awed by the presence of these battle-hardened warriors to complain of the depletion of their scarce foodstocks, and kept their grumbles until after the strangers departed.

At first cock-crow, some hours before dawn, a posse of soldiers from the Shaftesbury garrison arrived to escort the party on the last five miles of the journey. Their shouts of greeting awoke them all, and Æthelgifu offered aloud a fervent prayer to the pantheon of Saxon saints that they would all arrive safely in their new home. The other women chorused their Amen, and were reminded of the importance of the moment — probably the last journey of their lives before the gates of the new abbey would close behind them.

They reached the eastern end of the hilltop as light broke around them, although diffused through a thin mist brought on by the chill of the night. Late March sunshine would soon clear the mist, leaving only the surrounding vales shrouded in white mist-clouds until those too were burnt off. Only then would the viewer see over to the distant hills and ridges to both north and south and, in sharp detail, the intervening farms, fields and forests.

But now, while vision was still indistinct, hearing was intensified, all sounds carrying clearly in the still air. The party passed through the guarded opening in a palisade that ran across the width of the hilltop, from north at Tout Hill, to south. Edward acknowledged the sentries as they saluted the Aetheling. The clip-clop of horses' hooves of the arrival party rang on the stony surface of the main road, known as Bimport, which ran westwards from the Tout Hill entrance along the spine of the promontory. These sounds were joined by the clanking, creaking wheels of the carts and the baaing of the sheep previously grazing beside the roadway but now looking up curiously at the passing cavalcade. The new-born lambs ran to the safety of their mothers and dogs barked as heralds of the newcomers.

A newly-constructed fence and the backs of a series of low, thatched buildings screened the enclosure on their left from the travellers as they rode westwards. But Æthelgifu's full attention was on the sounds and smells coming from it. Wafting in the still air was the smell of wood fires filtering through roofs of thatch or wooden tiles, and the din of the clashes of iron pounding on iron, or wood being sawn and chopped. Cockerels crew, imposing their imperium over their various harems, and geese hissed. Other voices, those of people calling to each other while working or passing, and pigs and donkeys greeting the dawn, declared that the business of diurnal life had resumed. The abbey's horses stabled alongside the road neighed on hearing hooves on the cobbles, but the incoming steeds were too weary to respond.

What Æthelgifu was hearing brought on that same feeling of dread she had tried hard to master over the past few days. Not just the idea, the mental image, of an abbey — but she now apprehended the concrete reality of it. She was the daughter of a king but had never before exercised any authority. For all her life she had been obedient to superiors. Subservience had been drilled into her, enforced by beatings and other punishments. Now all those people who lived and worked beyond that wooden wall, as well as all the women bound to the religious life, would be obliged to obey her every command — as abbess. How would she know what to do and how should she deport herself? Abbess Mildritha had been her only role model, the only abbess she had known. Must she be like that — commanding, forbidding, always serious and quick to find faults? Or could she rule in altogether another way?

The small arrival party of escorting soldiers and the excited nuns passed groups of farm workers — churls and slaves — who had been released from a pair of great gates set into another palisade which transected the road further to the west. They were on their way to the path down Tout Hill on the northern side of the central road, or to the equally steep southern path. Once in the valleys they would take up their oxen and freemartins, attach them to ploughs and lead them to the fields for an exhausting day's work. These labourers now stopped to stare at the newcomers. Some of the escorting soldiers they knew well, others were warriors they had not seen before. As Edward approached, they recognised him to be a person of the highest rank, with a fine embroidered cloak, bronze and silver helmet and shining silver sword hilt. They dutifully bowed low, awed and honoured to have seen such an ealdorman at such close range.

When they realised that the women following the

escort must be the religious Handmaids they had been expecting, they knew the new Abbess of Shaftesbury must be among them, and called out for a blessing as she passed. Æthelgifu responded by tracing the air with two fingers in the sign of a cross, and the labourers dropped their scythes and ale-skins, clutched their hats to their chests, and, falling on their knees, bowed their heads. Æthelgifu could not resist a little smile while her heart fluttered.

After about a hundred yards, the front riders reached the first of a series of two defensive ditches at right angles from the road to the ridge where the land fell sharply to the north. These ditches were studded with sturdy pointed poles shoved into the earth at close intervals along their length. Any attacking force from the east would be funnelled into the first narrow guarded gateway on Bimport. The two soldiers on duty there nodded to their mounted colleagues, allowing them to pass unchallenged.

Not far beyond lay the second defence ditch, similar to the first but extending fully to the southern drop. Upon the mound created from the ditch was a palisade made of tall tree-trunks, their tops sharpened to points. This sturdy stockade encircled the burh. Right around it, about four feet below the top and on the inside, ran a platform from where lookouts could see for miles. Facing east was an impressive two-storey tower below which a pair of vast gates opened onto Bimport. The last of the labourers, passing through them, stood to watch, but Edward's party did not intend to go as far as the burh. Across from the first ditch-defence, and parallel with the road, was another wooden gate tower, though lower and less impressive than the burh's. This was the entrance to the abbey enclosure. The leading riders turned into it and the others followed. As they did, it seemed that all life within the compound froze in silence. The two gate-keepers bowed throughout the entrance procession, even when one of the cartwheels got caught momentarily on the frame of a gate and much jostling was needed to release it.

The party rode towards the spacious yard before the largest of the wooden thatched buildings, the Mead, or Great Hall, while Æthelgifu swept the scene with her eyes. Rectangular buildings of timber, or plaster over mud and wattle – similar to the imposing central one, but in varying smaller sizes – were scattered around the enclosure. Newly constructed, their thatches were still brightly straw-coloured, as yet undarkened by smoke and weathering.

One wooden building roofed with wooden tiles, further away and to their left, was marked by a large wooden cross standing before it and a scaffold protruding from its roof from which hung a large iron bell with an attached long rope. Some of the buildings had thatched or tiled roofs almost reaching down to the ground on either long side. The roofs of others stopped a few feet from the ground, allowing for narrow side windows with wattle shutters to keep out the cold night air. Hens, geese and goats roamed at will, while from some of the larger huts animal sounds indicated that they contained confined livestock of various sorts.

At the doorways of most of the buildings stood men, women and children, attired in simple peasant costume, undyed or plaid woollen tunics and plain wool leggings with cross garters on the men, and longer tunics and cloth headgears for the women.

They stood still, eagerly scanning the arrival of the new community of Handmaids, and were excited to see the noble band of warriors accompanying them. Small children hid behind their mothers' skirts, and dogs stopped chasing cats and chickens to watch the scene.

Æthelgifu had barely time to take in her surroundings, as her attention was drawn to two important personages, a familiar female one in religious habit, and a male, an obvious grandee, clothed in a tunic and cloak of the finest quality. They stood together in front of steps leading up to the open doors of the Great Hall, ready to receive the arrivals. Behind them stood an awkward row of low-born ragged servants and slaves, heads bowed and feet shuffling.

"My Lady Prioress, Master Reeve, Chad," acknowledged the senior officer of the Shaftesbury military escort with a slight bow to both. "Here are the holy Handmaids from your old abbey, with the Lord Edward and his men."

He and his men then turned their horses about and withdrew, while the servants rushed forward to help each of the Handmaids to dismount or the older ones to clamber down from the carts. Edward's men waited to see all the women safely taken in hand by those who had arrived a few days earlier, while supervising the servants unloading the carts.

Mistress Edith, the elderly Prioress from Wimborne, made direct for Æthelgifu and took both the girl's hands into her own bony ones. "Welcome, dear Sister," she enthused, beaming widely, "I do hope your journey here was comfortable. You're good and early too! Come in, come in, warm yourself and break your fast. We have bread newly baked and still warm. Come in!"

Æthelgifu smiled inwardly. Never had she known the strict and bossy Mother Edith behave in such a friendly way to her. She allowed herself to be led into the Great Hall, waving to her female companions to follow. Suddenly, she darted past them back to the outside again for a last goodbye with her brother, who had dismounted to converse with the well-dressed man of the welcoming party.

"Sister, this is Master Chad. Father appointed him to be reeve for you here. He it is who will administer royal rule and law in your lands. If you need anything, he's the man to go to."

"Indeed so, dear lady. I am at your service in all things."

"Delighted to meet you, Master Chad. I trust we shall work together well."

The older man moved away, towards the hall, while Æthelgifu and Edward embraced. Then the brother asked his sister for a blessing. She drew a small sign of the cross on his forehead and, with choking voice, bade God be with him. The Atheling turned quickly to his horse, hoping his sister did not notice a tear dewing his eye. He mounted and led his men, impatient as they were to be off, to their quarters in the adjoining burh, where bread, ale and warmth awaited. Chad bowed low to Æthelgifu, although genuine humility was not one of his usual attributes, and respectfully followed her into the Hall.

Moments later, chunks of hot buttered bread in hand and with beakers of weak ale beside them, Æthelgifu with her sisters-in-religion huddled on benches as close to the fire pit as they could get, thawing feet and hands after their chilly dawn journey.

A sudden clapping gained the attention of the gathered community. Chad then introduced himself to all, standing with feet apart and thumbs hooked into his finely-tooled leather belt, while Mother Edith stood beside him with, for her, an abnormally broad smile. He delivered his address to the company in a commanding voice, the piggy eyes in his red round face scanning the audience.

"Ladies, Handmaids of the Lord, I hope your journey here was uneventful — no wolves, or, God-forbid, Danes on your path?" he guffawed in an attempt to create an atmosphere of good humour. "You have come to what is to be your new home. It is more humble than you are used to with your fine stone abbey at Wimborne, but have patience, dear Ladies. These rough wooden buildings will soon be replaced by stone. King Alfred has given me instructions and the funding to see to it, and we'll be joined by Brother Grimbald from France. He knows all the architecture of the mighty abbeys in Europe and will see that this one at Shaftesbury will be no less great. After all, we have the King's own daughter to lead us and show that an abbey for women, the first great religious house in the land just for the weaker sex, can be as famous and important as any of their European counterparts."

Æthelgifu was glad that the man's attention was suddenly diverted from his audience. Two tousle-haired young men, at an age just short of full maturity, approached the fire-pit and waited to be invited to speak.

"Ah, my sons, Alwyn and Edwin." Deep bows from the youths, slight head-inclines from the women.

Then the older youth spoke, addressing the elderly standing nun, "Mother Prioress, the Lord Wulfsige, Bishop of Sherborne, has arrived and awaits you in the chapel."

The younger one turned to the reeve, "Father, the masons and quarrymen you were expecting have arrived and await you outside. They said you will show them where they are to work and where to live."

Having delivered their message, the youths withdrew, first bowing, then allowing the Prioress to go before them as she bustled her way outside and over the muddy ground to the chapel.

"Well, you see, until the monk Grimbald arrives, I am in charge of these workmen," Chad explained to his guests. "I expect the good Brother later today, coming with the King's party from Winchester. Great scholar, Master Grimbald, apparently. A musician as well. Humble man — turned down the offer to be the Archbishop of Canterbury. Can't think why."

Chad paused to drink, then decided to lecture the weary women further, considering, not entirely correctly, that their former lives spent within the cloister prevented them from knowing what went on in the world.

"This burh", he pointed through the doorway towards the town, "was built about eight years ago, as soon as your father, madam, the king, made peace with the Danes." He gave a slight bow towards Æthelgifu. "It is one of several such fortified townships, on hilltops like this one or using the remains of old Roman sites. They provide defences throughout Wessex, and this one gives protection to all the people living around and within it."

Æthelgifu had known all this, as had the others, but somehow the man ignored their nods and yawns. He continued, spreading his arm wide to indicate the extent of the place.

"Your abbey here was started at the King's request just last year, which is when I arrived. I'd been serving your father in the court at Winchester, but really don't mind coming here, despite it not being so busy or important, or even finished. Anyway, we started by levelling the ground and felling trees from the hillsides."

Some of the waiting masons peered in at the entrance, wondering what was keeping the reeve. They heard him declare, "So we had plenty of timber for building and fuel but also we have a good view of any Danes attempting to approach. While all the forests in the valleys could hide an approaching army, they'd have a job clambering unseen up these slopes! So you can sleep safely, my ladies! Well now, when you have warmed up and are ready, you'll find my sons just outside. They're waiting to show you around and, if you need anything, just ask them or Mother Edith. The Sisters who came with her, you know them of course, are unpacking the carts and they will let you know where all your things are being taken. Good morning, Ladies."

After another draught of ale, Chad bowed slightly and strolled out to meet the masons and quarrymen.

CHAPTER 3
PREPARING FOR THE BIG DAY

ÆTHELGIFU AND HER NUNS spent the morning exploring the buildings in the compound, often giggling together, heady with excitement. A few were silent, dismayed at the primitive nature of the wooden buildings. They were so unlike the stone magnificence of Wimborne Abbey, with its two cloisters and many sturdy structures. The new abbey was indeed far from the complex sophistication of the great Continental abbeys such as that of St Gall. Here, apart from the Great, or Mead Hall, there was a modest series of buildings of all sizes arranged around the precinct. Close up to the surrounding fence were the houses of the workers, each shared by at least one family and the animals they personally owned. The abbey's beasts and fowl were housed in a great byre near the entrance, alongside the long granary, as yet almost empty. Once the tithes were collected in the form of produce from the lands given to the abbey, it would fill. There were a few months to go before the grain harvest so the granary was currently in use storing the few sacks of flour, dried peas and beans, and racks of root vegetables – much of it brought from Wimborne.

Then there were the workshops and other functional buildings, such as the combined brewery and bakery, the linen house, the dairy, the kitchen close to the Hall, and the infirmary, which was at a distance from the other buildings, to prevent the spread of infection. Also distanced was the latrine, with a pit beneath it which would be emptied regularly and the contents used to fertilise the fields. The chapel, with its bell and cross, was prominent, with an adjacent house for the family of the mass-priest, a young man personally selected by King Alfred for his scholarship and piety.

Æthelgifu learned which was to be her own simple house, so newly built that the firepit had not been in use and the underside of the roof not yet blackened. A similar mud-and-wattle structure nearby was where guests were to be lodged. She felt a little surge of pleasure to think of having a house of her own, having known only dormitory accommodation.

Edwin and Alwyn proved entertaining guides,

commenting on the buildings and inhabitants with witty observations, making the younger newcomers laugh even more.

Æthelgifu broke away from her Sisters to approach some of the workpeople in their workshops and homes. Her nerves subsided somewhat at their shy smiles and awkward bows as she greeted them.

"It can't be too bad," she thought, "if these people are so pleasant. It seems likely they'll be easy to work with."

She had an encouraging word in the linen house with Sister Fritha who had arrived with Mistress Edith's advance party. She was supervising the sweeping of the floor by a young red-haired girl and holding an armful of straw and sweet herbs to lay down over the earth floor once the old and dusty ones were cleared.

Æthelgifu noticed the young sweeping girl was dressed in simple Viking style.

"This is Skadi," Sister Fritha explained, seeing Æthelgifu's slight frown. "She is Danish, one of the half-dozen slaves sent from the burh to work for us. Four are Danes and a couple are Welsh. They're all trustworthy, so don't worry about them. Hard-workers too. But most of the other layfolk here are free-born churls, all drafted in from next door or recruited from the villages."

Æthelgifu felt a chill of apprehension at the

thought of hostile Danish and Welsh slaves at loose in the enclosure, but this girl, of no more than twelve or thirteen years of age, looked to be no threat. The Saxon princess smiled at her and received a grin in return.

Fritha stood still, unsure how to address the young abbess-to-be. 'Mother' would be the official form, despite the difference in age, once consecrated. Until then, what to say? Æthelgifu sensed the unease. There was nothing actively to dislike about Sister Fritha as there was so little there to react to at all. She had sublimated her personality so completely that Æthelgifu was pricked with irritation whenever she came across her. Held up as a model of obedience and piety, Fritha glided around in the shadows, doing whatever was asked of her without demur. No, the novice Æthelgifu had once said to herself, I cannot, will not, ever be like that. Such passivity is cowardice, not a virtue. Now, as she looked at the humble nun, she realised this woman would be offering to her, Æthelgifu, the total obedience of a subject to a king, or a believer to God. A shiver ran down her, so she simply nodded and left.

She could not join the others in the giggling group. She was different. No longer an equal, sharing their jokes, whispering their secrets, fearing the rebukes of superiors. Falling out of friendship, making up after quarrels, warning each other, learning how to cope with their developing female bodies, helping each other with their studies and covering for each other when blamed – such was the society of the young Handmaids. All would now be closed to her. She would soon be the person whom they dreaded in the doling out of penances. She would be the one determining their work-roles and measuring the results. She, the abbess, would be the ultimate arbitrator — and not just of these religious women and child oblates, nor just of all the workforce within the abbey's boundary – but of all the tenants, churls and slaves, and even thegns, upon the abbey's extensive landholdings. Her knees would barely sustain her weight, so she made for the chapel, to sit on a bench with her back to the wall.

After inspecting the grounds, the other newcomers took themselves to the rim of the southern slope, admiring the views of the layers of hills and fertile valleys. At the tolling of the bell, they turned and assembled in the chapel for prayer, where they noticed Æthelgifu was sitting, head lowered, in the gloom. They could not see her tears.

At the end of the office of sext, as the sun had risen to its height, Prioress Edith summoned all the sisters back to the Great Hall, to await the imminent arrival of the royal party. The Bishop of Sherborne and Master Chad were already awaiting as the excited Sisters joined them with a pretence of modest formality. Now Æthelgifu's blue eyes sparkled and cheeks burned with emotion. She could not stop smiling, for she would soon see her beloved parents once more – after years of being apart.

After an hour or two of excited waiting, the townspeople lining Bimport were alerted by lookout scouts to the arrival of the royal party. Their cheers reached inside the Great Hall. When the party of mounted warriors, led by the king himself, passed by them, they fell silent, bowing in respect. "We have seen the king today," they said, in tones of awe.

The courtyard in front of the Great Hall soon filled with a chaotic crowding of people and horses. The Prioress and Chad the reeve greeted the royal guests while Æthelgifu watched from the entrance, her heart fluttering. Servants and slaves held the steaming horses as the party of ealdormen, thegns and monks dismounted. The mounts of King Alfred and of his wife, Lady Ealhswith, were tended by Alwyn and Edwin, while their riders nodded in acknowledgement to Prioress Edith and Reeve Chad, but their eyes were looking out for their daughter. When they saw Æthelgifu, they smiled at the tall young woman she had become, and dismounted.

Æthelgifu ran to embrace her parents – tears glistening on the cheeks of mother and daughter, while her warrior father had to blink several times to restrain his. Bringing herself to a sudden stop before them, she dropped a full curtsey. Her father raised her and hugged her warmly, as then did her smiling mother. After a suitable interval, the Prioress stepped forward to take charge of Æthelgifu while Chad invited the king and his wife to go with him into the Great Hall. Their daughter remained, with Edith's hand upon her arm, staring intensely into the dark doorway, impatient to join her kin inside.

After a short time of conference between the royal parents, the Bishop of Sherborne, and the reeve, first the bishop and then Chad emerged. The bishop took Edith towards the chapel, while Chad invited Æthelgifu to replace him in the hall. She wasted no time and soon the three of them were seated, the teenager facing the adults across the trestle, her hands in theirs.

Ealhswith was almost speechless. She had had so much she wanted to say, but for a time could not find the words. It had been several years since she had seen this daughter, not since the sickly, rather timid little girl with long blond plaits had been handed over to the Handmaids. Now a self-possessed young woman sat before her, hair suitably covered in a yellow wimple and eyes shining with excitement and with a ready smile. From her hours outdoors tending the herb garden in Wimborne and gathering wild plants for use in the infirmary and elsewhere, she looked healthy and robust — and happy. That last provided Ealhswith with the greatest consolation. She had worried that the great step ahead of the girl, of ruling this new establishment with all its lands and tenants, would be grudgingly undertaken, as a mere act of obedience.

Alfred, too, had been concerned about the fulfilment of his promise to God to found abbeys were he granted victory over the heathen Danish forces. Would installing his daughter at the head of this one be at the expense of her happiness? Would she rather crave marriage and motherhood? He relaxed as he saw now that he need not have worried.

The three exchanged family news although Alfred abruptly cut the conversation away from the subject of his health problems – digestive and abdominal in the main – in consideration for his daughter's peace of mind. Instead, he briefly related accounts of some of his travels and successes. He told her of his two journeys to Rome when a child, and how the Pope confirmed him and anointed him as a future king, despite having three older brothers who would fulfil that role before him. He also recalled winning a beautiful book of poetry before he was six which his mother had offered to whichever child could learn it first. He recited the whole of it having heard it only a few times. He treasured it still.

"Come now, Alfred", chided Ealhswith, "tell our daughter of more recent happenings."

Æthelgifu was delighted to hear that two years earlier, after its destruction by the Danes, her father had restored the old Roman town of London to Mercia, now under his overlordship. He had led a large force of his Wessex countrymen to assist their old enemies, men of Mercia. The Mercians too acclaimed him as their lord. She felt so proud of her father, and pleased at the obvious delight of her Mercian mother at this development.

"Talking of Mercia, Father, please tell me about my dear sister Athelflad. Since you had married her to the Mercian Lord Ethelred I have heard nothing from her. How do the Mercians take to her as a Wessex woman?"

"Don't forget that through me," commented her mother, "she could claim some Mercian blood in her veins." Ealhswith was always sensitive about her roots, feeling that to be Mercian was in no way inferior to being Wessex-born. The enmity between their people was ridiculous in her view, as they shared so much and differed so little.

Alfred smiled. "Do I detect a hint of disapproval, daughter, that I sent my eldest into hostile territory? You need not worry. She seems to be a popular figure in the Court there. She's about to give birth any day. A strong son would cement the bond between our two people."

"Even a daughter," added his wife with a sudden

frown. "Let's just hope both mother and baby do well. We'll send you word about her news. Indeed, I shall see you are informed of any event in which you may be interested. And we shall want to know how you are doing here. If you need anything, anything at all, you must send a messenger. Winchester is not so very far away, after all. A day's journey or two at most."

Æthelgifu thanked her parents and swore to do all she could to be worthy of her responsible position. Alfred felt a surge of happiness, perhaps more than at any other time since his great victory at Edington ten years before. Within his mind he could see that part of his vision, his sense of destiny, was now to be served by his own daughter — in restoring the True Faith to the land. Christianity, with its civilising culture of care and hospitality, had been largely lost through savage waves of heathen Danish invasions. Now, through such an abbey as this, the virtues endowed through the grace of God, would return to the land and, with God's favour, the Saxon kingdoms would one day be united. In God's time even the Norsemen would be converted and live peaceably under Saxon rule. If not, they must surely be expelled from the land. That was the deal. Victory in battle for Saxons, Christianity restored for God. There was no shame in exchanging terms with God — after all, did not Abraham haggle with the Almighty over the number of survivors of the righteous in doomed Sodom?

The family gathering, precious for being short and good-natured, was ended by the sound of the chapel bell, summoning the soon-to-be abbess to Vespers. At the same time, her brother Edward entered the hall and replaced Æthelgifu who, for the first time in her life, was reluctant to attend a church service. But Edward and his parents had plenty to discuss, despite his frequent presence with them at court. As senior atheling, or heir apparent, he could not be sure of the succession after his father's death. That would be decided by the ealdormen at the Witanagemot, so he needed to impress everybody with his attention to martial arts, politics and diplomacy – a heavy agenda for a youth in his teen years.

When Æthelgifu entered the chapel for Vespers, she saw that the Prioress had given up her presiding place, facing the community, to the bishop and an abbot, who were flanked by a monk and a mass-priest. Instead, she stood in the centre of the congregation of women, and made a place next to her for Æthelgifu. Women whom Æthelgifu had not yet met were standing among those she knew well, and a few elderly women were seated on benches set along the walls.

"These must be the daughters and widows come

with my parents from Winchester," she surmised, wondering if she would find the courage within her to command these strangers and form them into a happy and prayerful community. Her mind was so full she heard little of the psalms and bible readings intoned by the clergymen, reciting from two massive books, a Latin Psalter and a Lectionary respectively, resting on carved wooden lecterns before them.

After the service, Æthelgifu remained in the chapel while the others filed out. She stayed there until Compline, when the women returned alone and in silence and conducted the short service of readings and prayers without the aid of clerics. Then, led out by the Prioress, they left Æthelgifu alone again.

She spent the long, cold hours of night in praying, her hands held up beside her head, palms upwards, in the accepted position for prayer. She recited remembered biblical verses, mulling them over slowly, savouring the words and seeking deeper meanings. From time to time she looked up favourite passages in the beautifully handwritten and illustrated Lectionary, translating the original Vulgate in her head into English. The two liturgical volumes had been brought with great care from Wimborne, regarded as precious treasures, both in content and as artefacts. At one time she simply stood, watching the candles flicker and burn out, leaving her with just the glow of moonlight through the narrow windows and doorway. She wondered how many bees had each candle taken to create and how God must bless their industry, knowing their labours would lighten holy places such as this.

She sometimes knelt on the earthy floor, until the damp seeped into her knees and made her shiver. Then she would stand and walk around in slow circles, flapping her arms against her sides for warmth. Other times she just stood, feet apart for balance as sleepiness made her sway occasionally. She resisted the temptation to sit on the benches against the walls, as fearing she would drop off to sleep were she to do so. And so the night went on — not always silently, as loud raucous laughter and shouting from the nearby town carried through the still chill air. The freemen from the town and the visitors, royal and warrior, were feasting and drinking in the Great Hall of the burh of Shaftesbury, celebrating the arrival of the esteemed guests with the consumption of great quantities of ale, mead and wine. The king absented himself when the behaviour of some of the heavy drinkers became too abandoned, as he disapproved of drunkenness. The more astute and sensitive of his followers did likewise, but the others continued their loud revelry into the early hours.

The only break in Æthelgifu's night vigil was with the arrival of a girl of about thirteen, barefoot and dressed in a rough undyed woollen dress gathered with a cord belt. She entered quietly and only by coughing gently did she take the attention of the princess.

"Oh, who are you?" asked a startled Æthelgifu, roused from deeply meditating on the surprising ways in which God uses young women, such as the young peasant-girl Mary, betrothed to a carpenter, to be the Virgin Mother of the Blessed Lord Jesus. Now, in a far humbler way, God is using herself.

"Oh, I'm sorry, my Lady. I didn't mean to disturb you, but Mistress Prioress told me to bring you this shawl to keep you warm on such a chill night." As she handed it over, she added, "She also said that I was to be your personal servant, my lady, if you'll have me."

This took Æthelgifu by surprise and a little annoyance to have to take on the responsibility of another person, even one supposed to be a help, just at this time when she had so much to think about. However, she quickly collected herself, realising that in her new role in life she would be faced with many decisions and novelties to cope with, so had better begin now with a calmer manner.

"Of course — unless you do anything to cross me. What is your name?"

"I am Tild, daughter of Wigmund, one of the farriers here in Shaftesbury. Mistress Prioress has been training me in what I should do as your servant, my Lady, when you are the Abbess here."

"Good, that's fine, Tild. Go now and get your sleep. Leave me to my prayers, and, in future, do not disturb me with words when I am praying." She felt a pang of pity for the stricken child at this rebuke so early in the girl's service, so added, "It's all right this time, of course, Tild — as I spoke to you first. But usually, prayer is something that cannot be interrupted. I'll see you tomorrow. Tell Mistress Prioress that I thank her for her kindness. With this warm shawl I shall be quite snug in here."

CHAPTER 4
THE BIG DAY

MORNING EVENTUALLY dawned, and Æthelgifu felt hungry and very cold, even with the thick woollen shawl wrapped tightly around her. She knew she could not eat until after the service of her installation, but left the chapel to seek out in the Great Hall a draught of water to keep herself from fainting. Pure water drawn from the wells at the foot of the hill had been brought up to the abbey for just such a purpose. None of the religious women had taken food or drink since the simple refreshments when they had arrived the previous day. Now they sank great quantities of the cool refreshing liquid. Usually, it would have to be boiled and fermented into ale to be safe, but this was clean and fresh, and very welcome.

The sisters had spent the night in the Great Hall

at the abbey, sleeping on rows of wide wooden boards either side of the central fire. In the early morning they assembled these boards into the trestles upon with they and the guests would be served food after the special service. The high table, raised on a low plank dais and facing the entrance doors, was a permanent structure with fixed legs. This would be where the high-ranking diners sat, while the trestles ran in long rows at right angles to it at both ends.

The Office of Matins, at about two o'clock at night, had been dispensed with to allow Æthelgifu to pursue her solitary vigil in the chapel. But the sisters assembled there at dawn for Lauds, after refreshing themselves with drinking water, and remained in the chapel all morning. One of King Alfred's ingenious inventions was to mark a thick candle at intervals which determined the passing of each hour when lit. One such candle was usually kept alight in the house of the sacristan, to let her know when to toll the bell to summon the community to prayer. Until a sacristan was appointed, Prioress Edith kept it in her quarters and performed the service.

While remaining in the chapel, they broke their silent reflection to chant the Offices of Prime and Terce, after which, on this occasion came Mass. The mass-priest was a slender flaxen-haired young man with a magnificently bushy moustache with long ends that drooped below his jaw. In the short intervals between the services, the women left the chapel to visit the latrine hut or simply to warm up in the spring sunshine, walking quickly and taking deep draughts of clean air. The smoke given off by the candles that lit the small windowless chapel, and the number of unwashed bodies, made the air stale and frowsty. Some of the older women could not remain standing or kneeling, so retired to the benches ranged along the walls. The Prioress led the prayers of the Offices, making the most of her provisional position at the head of the community.

She and Æthelgifu left the chapel at mid-morning, after Terce. They went to the lodging close to the Great Hall, that its new mistress had visited the day before, the Abbess House. The door of it was open, and this time Æthelgifu could see a fire blazing within. Tild, her new maid, was standing by, smiling. Now the girl was shod in new leather shoes and wore an orange woollen peplos, a tubular dress over an undergarment of linen. Her hair was brushed and face and hands washed clean.

The Prioress withdrew, returning to the chapel for the midday Office of Sext, held especially early on this occasion. In the Abbess House, still smelling of new plaster and limewash, Tild helped Æthelgifu prepare herself for the forthcoming ceremony. She undid the old-fashioned brooches holding up her fine woollen peplos and removed the simple tight-sleeved linen underdress in which she had been travelling and spending the night. Then the garters holding up woollen leggings were untied and the articles rolled off. Last to go were the travel-pants, similar to those worn by monks when travelling, to be laundered and lent to any Sister who would be journeying somewhere.

Æthelgifu had bathed only a few months before, so now just washed her body in herbally scented water, which Tild brought to her in leather buckets. The biting cold of the water, while refreshing, was soon forgotten under the friction of the woollen towel with which she dried herself. Then Tild helped her on with robes that had been laid out over the straw-filled palliasse on her bed — clothes produced earlier by Æthelgifu's mother as a gift.

A clean long linen *gunna* was put on first, an undergown with ample folds on the sleeves, to be pulled over the hands in cold weather. Then the headdress, a soft pale-gold cloth, longer than a person's height, was placed over the head, around the face and wound around the neck, and held in place on her head by a golden circlet of a fine filigree design. Then Tild held up the heavy woollen blue ankle-length tunic and helped Æthelgifu place her arms through the sleeves with their bell-like opening at the elbow. With a wiggle of her shoulders, Æthelgifu drew the garment down over herself.

Embroidered red and gold-thread braid ran down both sides of the front seam and around both cuffs and the hem.

A loose girdle of similar braid went around it, dropping down on the right-hand side with some of the tunic gathered up over it. Fresh leggings were rolled on and held in position by garter ribbons, and a pair of fine black leather shoes completed the ensemble. Æthelgifu was ready to face all the attention she knew she would attract over the next few hours. A bell tolled.

Tild drew in her breath and caught her mistress's eye. The two young women smiled. The moment had come and, with a prayer for divine help on her lips and heartbeats thudding against her chest, Æthelgifu walked out across the yard and into the chapel.

The service of consecration and installation of the new abbess was conducted with great solemnity by Bishop Wulfsige of Sherborne. Standing before the altar, with his back to it until the Mass itself began, he was attended by the mass-priest, and two monks. One was introduced as Abbot John of the new abbey of Athelney, the twin foundation to this one, only for men, and Master Grimbald, a Frankish monk on temporary loan from the court at Winchester, where he was a valued adviser.

Seated on a raised chair facing them in central place was the new abbess, with the Handmaids, novices, and vowed women standing beside her. On her chest gleamed the silver pectoral cross presented to her to mark her new rank, similar to that of a bishop or an ealdorman. Though equal in status, her future contribution to the political life of the country was limited because of her sex.

Behind the religious women stood her proud parents and brother, as well as Cynehelm, the Thegn of Shaftesbury, and Chad the Reeve with his sons and two further monks from Athelney who possessed the only unsmiling faces of the assembly. Indeed, these two monks looked positively truculent, and muttered darkly to each other from time to time.

After the withdrawal of the clergy, monks and noble guests, Æthelgifu asked the ladies to remain. Exhaling a deep breath she relaxed her shoulders to calm her nerves, stood and turned to face them, to address her sisters for the first time as their abbess. She began by asking for their prayers and support, in exchange for her efforts in leading an establishment worthy of its dedication to the Virgin Mother of Christ.

Some of the professed Handmaids and vowesses she knew well, having been with them for years at Wimborne Abbey. Two of them, including Mistress Fritha, had been with the Prioress's advance party. She did not know the three new widows who would vow to live chaste and devout lives. While all the other women present were free-born members of the highest warrior classes, ealdormen or thegns, these widows may not have been so nobly born but had been wives of honoured warriors who had died in the service of Saxon Wessex. Another mature woman present was not a widow, but a married woman who had renounced her marital status, with her husband's consent.

Then there were several young women quite unknown to Æthelgifu, shy and nervous teenagers, who were to join the novitiate after a short period of postulancy. This introductory stage allowed them to see what would be involved in the religious life and whether they felt duly committed to it. They had been accompanied by their fathers in the royal party and brought generous dowries of lands and jewels with them. As novices, they would be formed in the spiritual life until they, like their sisters older in religion, make their vows of obedience, stability — to the community and the place in which they were now — and of *conservatio morum*, or 'conversion of manners'. This meant turning from worldly interests to those of the religious life.

Æthelgifu trembled a little at the thought of the onerous responsibility she now had of being the ultimate spiritual guide for these young women. Then she heard herself promising that there would be more such religious women — especially young ones who would become Handmaids.

"To receive new members, the community must be united and devout," Æthelgifu emphasised, feeling her confidence strengthening as she spoke. "Only by developing a good reputation will we be ensured of growth both in numbers and in individual piety. Any problems must be resolved openly and honestly – with no back-biting or malicious gossip. Prioress Edith will ensure the smooth daily running of the community as she has been doing magnificently for so long" – the lady blushed at this praise – "and I, as your Abbess, will preside with justice and mercy, as God would require me to do."

After these heartening words, the small community withdrew for a while, to reflect upon all that had been said in the chapel. They strolled in silence around the enclosure, alone or in twos and threes.

Meanwhile in the Great Hall, the tables were being prepared for the celebratory feast. Edwin and Alwyn were meant to be helping to set everything up, but spent most their time watching the two servant girls, who happened to be the prettiest in the town, draping the fine linens over the long top table. Instead of lending a hand, the lads made silly bantering jokes as the girls struggled to keep the cloths from creasing or falling off the table's edge.

One cloth ran the length of the table and hung right down, hiding the legs of the dignitaries. Another, on the seating side, just hung to the level of the diners' knees. The girls laid two more cloths, each reaching to the platform on the short side. Then these were topped by another which draped over the edges all round and finally, a drawer cloth was laid along the sitting-down edge. These two servants were used to the process, as they were also responsible for dressing the altar in the town's church in the same way. But that did not stop them pretending to get things slightly wrong so that they could giggle and flirt with the reeve's two boys.

Alwyn and Edwin waited until the girls had finished their task before placing chairs along one side of the top table, facing the trestles and the Great Door. They had already set long benches down by the trestle tables running at right angles from the top table, on either side of the firepit. Linen was not used on these trestles, but a bowl of salt was placed halfway down each, and platters and goblets indicated the place settings.

As the guests began to arrive and take their places, young male servants positioned themselves at side tables at strategic distances, each table provided with jugs of ale and mead, and flagons of water and bowls for hand washing, and towels. Meat-eating always greased the fingers of those feasting, however delicate their manners. When Æthelgifu and her procession of women entered, the general banter and laughter of those present subsided respectfully. Chad and his sons took it upon themselves to direct each lady to her place — Æthelgifu and the Prioress seated at the high table, the other religious women on the trestles, nearest to the top.

Then the whole assembly rose as King Alfred and Lady Ealhswith entered and took their places at the centre of the high table. Æthelgifu was seated at her father's right side, and the Bishop of Sherborne on her own right. Ealhswith, with Edward beside her on one side and the King on the other, was all smiles and contentment. She felt that today was one of the happiest of her life. Many other dignitaries, clergy and monks sat along the high table, while at the long trestles sat the monastic men and women, ealdormen and chosen warriors from the burh. The ealdormen could not stop watching their daughters, hoping that they would find contentment in this place, and bring honour to the family by their piety and devotion. Having a family member spending her life in prayer would surely provide divine help for her parents in this life and the next.

Before the food was brought in, there were speeches. At least liquid was unstintingly provided during them or the patience of the listeners would have been strained.

The king first welcomed everyone and bid them drink and feast well in celebration of this great day. Besides, on the next day, being Ash Wednesday, the great six-week fast of Lent would begin, leading up to Easter. He then listed the lands and income he was bestowing on this special abbey, a hundred hides to start with, and more to follow. He presented his personal gift to his daughter — a splendid nef, a decorated box containing the knife, spike and spoons brought to the table for each meal.

"For this abbey," he continued, "I donate a fine Latin Bible, and a richly jewelled finger-marker with which to read it without soiling the parchment. Although the Scriptures are here in Latin, my hope is that Shaftesbury Abbey scholars will translate it into our own language. Alas, only a pitiably few people these days, including many within the priesthood, can understand the Latin they recite daily."

The learned clerics at the table shook their heads in agreement, with sad expressions. "I deplore this!" the King declared animatedly, and the clergymen nodded. "In fact, I am writing a document to be sent throughout the land describing how to restore all the knowledge and culture that once graced this country and since has been forgotten."

A ripple of applause followed. The King warmed to his subject.

"All children shall be enabled to read and write in

English, and all those training to take Holy Orders shall be fluent in Latin too. I myself have been taking Latin lessons for the past year, from Brother Asser here."

He turned to address the monk, who blushed to be singled out.

"Good Brother Asser, not only will you help to create a centre of learning here, but will, one day, be Bishop of Sherborne — after the retirement of our esteemed Bishop Wolfsige."

He smiled over to that elderly churchman and made a slight bow. Ealhswith gave her husband's sleeve an inconspicuous little tug, to remind him to move on from this subject over which he somewhat obsessed. Alfred then cleared his throat as he remembered the remainder of his speech.

"Ah, yes," Alfred looked down at a scrap of parchment in his hand in which he had inscribed some notes. "Now, here, these humble wooden buildings you see around you will soon be replaced by fine stone ones, and I shall pay for it all. Especially that dingy little chapel — that must be the first to go." Æthelgifu nodded vigorously at that.

"Allow me to introduce Master Grimbald here in whom I have given charge of the building project." That esteemed monk stood to receive the invited applause.

"This very hill provides an ample quarry of

greensand stone, and the best masons will be deployed in all haste, I swear," asserted the King. Warming to his theme, he went on,

"Just as the battlefield provides martyrs for Christ, so the great new abbey church here will be where noble women can lead self-sacrificial lives for the King of Heaven and the good of all the living and the noble dead. The heathen Danes may have been sent by God to punish us Saxons for our lack of faith, and these vile creatures have destroyed or dispersed great Christian communities. Ely, Wareham and Wilton abbeys have all suffered, but one day, if God wills, all Danes will, like King Guthrum of East Anglia, be converted to the True Faith through the prayers of such men and women as at Athelney and here, at Shaftesbury."

Resounding cheers met this speech, with even Æthelgifu and her women voicing their approval and banging their knife-handles on the table.

Then the king made an announcement that caused great astonishment and intense delight.

"Five years ago," he said quietly, so that all would listen intently, "Pope Marinus sent me a gift from Rome. The holiest one possible".

He paused, to heighten the effect.

"A fragment of the True Cross — wood from the cross on which our Saviour hung." A collective gasp was heard throughout the Hall.

"Found by the Empress Helena, the Holy Cross has been divided into small sections, even splinters. One of these sections is even now in my possession, kept in a reliquary within this golden casket."

A servant lifted an object covered in a fine crimson linen cloth from a side table behind the diners and handed it to the king. Alfred placed it on the table and withdrew the cloth to another collective gasp.

"I am donating the precious relic and its reliquary within the casket here to this abbey at Shaftesbury, to be displayed at suitable times upon the altar of the stone church which will be built to be worthy of it."

The casket was an object of incredible beauty — gold worked with inlays of coloured Italian glass, Indian garnets and other semiprecious stones, with crosses and fish motifs. He decided not to open it at this time, so recovered it and handed it to Chad, who immediately left the Hall with it.

After King Alfred sat, to the loud applause of beefy fists thumping upon the tables, the elderly Bishop Wulfsige of Sherborne tottered to his feet and welcomed this new neighbouring religious community with its gracious abbess, and promised as a gift all the salt they would ever need, brought by cart from Sherborne Cathedral's salt land at Axmouth on the coast.

The Abbott of Malmesbury Abbey, a rubicund

fellow with a wide smile and seeming always to be at the point of bursting out laughing, next stood and welcomed the new community, promising some of his most gifted monks to come to share their deep learning and knowledge of Scripture and theology with the Sisters. Glancing at the previous speaker, he spoke apparently jokingly,

"The famous Aldhelm, one of my predecessors at Malmesbury, was — as you know — also the Bishop of Sherborne." That raised a laugh, although the elderly Bishop Wulfsige looked far from happy.

"Well," the abbot continued, "he was the author of a collection of letters on a very relevant subject, '*De Virginitate*' — sending advice to a community of Handmaids in Essex. We have kept his side of the correspondence, but not the ladies' letters, as it would not be proper. Anyway, I shall always be available to advise these dear Sisters in similar fashion should they so require."

Then it was the turn of Abbot John of Athelney, a man whose expression could curdle milk. He was reknowned as a scholar and as a man of high intelligence, formerly a soldier before entering religious life to pursue the company of books and scrolls — rather than of human society, which he tended to find contemptible.

He donated a valuable Psalter, produced by the monks of Rheims, his and Grimbald's previous abbey, and promised the services of the best scribes in Athelney, Pepin and Mark, to stay behind to instruct those of the sisters skilled in calligraphy.

Cynehelm, Thegn of Shaftesbury, then stood and, less accustomed to public oratory than were the previous speakers, spoke with jerky utterance in an embarrassed manner.

"To you, worthy and holy ladies, we, the soldiers and menfolk in general in our little town, right next door here, we, uh, we pledge our support and assistance. Don't you ever be afraid, Ladies, we're here for your protection!" That drew loud cheers and table-thumping from the audience, even from the King himself.

Encouraged, he continued, "And, er, we give to you something our carpenters have been working on ever since we heard you be coming — three mighty great weaving looms and all the carded wool you need to see you through until your own sheep be ready."

A voice from one of the trestles called out, "And the plants. Don't forget them!"

"Oh, aye, I was forgetting. That's it. We've got a cart-load of herbs — all sorts — we're going to let you have, in the root, so you can get your garden going straight away and start healing the sick, and all."

With that the rugged warrior resumed his seat, relieved that his ordeal was over. "I'd rather face an army of the heathen Danish with one arm tied behind my back, than have to do that again," he muttered, smiling, to his neighbour at the table, "and with the King listening – phew!"

After that, a stream of servants filed into the hall from the adjoining kitchen, placing around the tables spit-roasts of beef, mutton and venison, goose, chicken and pigeon, with platefuls of hardboiled eggs, cheeses, bowls of hot soups of stewed beef and barley and others of milky honeyed oat puddings. Before each diner were placed round flat 'plates' of bread on which the meat juices would soak. Then, last to be placed along the tables, were the saucers of sauces, into which the diners could dip their food. Barely had the food been placed, and a short Latin blessing on it been voiced by the Bishop, than each guest reached out with their spikes to skewer a good portion of the delicious food before them.

Some of the hunting and guard dogs which had until then lain quietly under the tables near the warmth of the fire, now stood, drooling and whimpering for morsels to fall — or be surreptitiously handed down to them. Æthelgifu was hungry but her stomach felt it was held in a vice. However, after a goblet of wine and a morsel of meat she began to relax, and then her appetite returned, and she enjoyed the unprecedented array of succulent delights before her.

Baldric, Alfred's favourite scop (minstrel), from Winchester, a tall clean-shaven man with a long face like a horse's, began fingering his nine-stringed harp. His song, in praise of Saxon warriors triumphing over heathen hordes, was hardly heard above the din of chatter and scraping plates. As empty goblets were refilled, the noise increased until the minstrel's song was utterly submerged. The sound of good cheer instead filled the hall, from the tinkling laughter of some of the ladies, to great guffaws and loud brays from many of the men, with the occasional dog-bark for good measure.

When no-one could eat more, the servants, mostly hired for the occasion from the town, trooped in again to remove the platters and bowls. Alwyn and Edwin gathered the bread plates, those that had not been gnawed or chewed, into sacks to take to distribute to the poor that evening. Other nutritious leftovers would also be distributed to them, once the servants had taken their share.

The king clapped for silence and, that attained, gestured to the scop to perform his specially commissioned ballad. All listened attentively as the lanky minstrel sang. He praised the king, of course, celebrating the peace achieved by his masterful leadership. Then he lauded the lovely daughter, the holy abbess who would rule her little realm as full of skill, honour and piety as did her father over the land of Wessex and would one day over the whole of England itself. While the king's first-born daughter, Athelflad, was bringing new bodily life into the world over in Mercia, expecting to give birth any day, so too new spiritual life was coming to Shaftesbury with this house of godly women.

After the thumping applause died down, the King rose and, taking his lady by the hand, left the Hall. The rest followed, some taking unsteady steps after too much alcohol. Outside, as dusk was falling, the women who were to remain in the abbey took their tearful leave of their families. Æthelgifu was no less upset at having to say farewell to her mother, father and brother. After much hugging and kissing, the Sisters then waved to those departing, and reluctantly returned to the Great Hall to assist in the transformation from dining hall to dormitory.

The clerical men retired to their guest quarters within the enclosure to await the bells for the Offices, while the royal party and other laity made their way to the burh, from which they would leave next morning at daybreak on their way to Athelney and thence to Mercia. The Lady Ealhswith carried with her a letter from Æthelgifu to her older sister, in which she prayed for the latter's safe delivery of her baby, and hoped for a letter in return.

CHAPTER 5

TILD

ÆTHELGIFU FELT AN EMPTINESS, a deep loneliness inside her over the next few days. She knew that she may never see her parents, and perhaps not even Edward, ever again. Their lives, embroiled in politics and fighting, and always on the move, were so remote from hers, now she had arrived in her final home. But also she was bereft of the company of her friends, the young Sisters with whom she had grown up. They had shared one another's secret thoughts and dreams. Some remained in Wimborne, others she could see daily, but not now join. She was no longer one of them, but their superior, with great powers over their lives. Now even the Prioress, who had always controlled every aspect of her life, was to be subject in all important matters to herself.

While brooding on her new isolated position, she found there was one person she could talk with in an easy way — young Tild. Not subjected to the disciplines and politics of the religious community, Tild brought with her the air of the world outside. To Tild, Æthelgifu spoke of her suddenly transformed status, from humble and rather junior sister, at the beck and call of first her novice mistress and then the prioress, to the heady height of community leader. Tild replied with an anecdote of her own. In the battle of Edington her uncle was one of the shield men, whose job was to protect the warriors by keeping the shield wall steady, opening it at the command for the warriors to break through and fight, then run back behind the wall. Tild's uncle saw one of the best and bravest warriors about to be struck from behind, so he picked up an axe that had been dropped earlier and was at his feet, broke from the shield line and slew the Dane before he could injure the Saxon. This Eorlderman then turned to him and promoted him on the spot to become one of the elite fighters.

"Mmm," said Æthelgifu quietly, "but he earned his new role."

"Yes, my lady Abbess, but you be the king's daughter — that'd be enough!"

Æthelgifu chuckled, delighted by the girl's simplicity. Tild spoke of her friend, the Danish slave bought by Prioress Edith from Cynehelm, the warrior thegn of the burh. Skadi had been brought as a young child to the burh just after it was built, with several other Danish children, orphaned after their parents had been killed in skirmishes in Kent. They were given tasks which increased in difficulty as they grew older.

"The one that Skadi really hates," said Tild, laughing, "is working the plunger in the butter churn — so boring and repetitive, or worse still, turning the heavy stone querns to grind wheat and barley grains into flour. Of course, when she was little she mainly just had to gather wood for the fires."

Æthelgifu remembered also having to do that, along with her sisters, before she was sent to the nunnery. Fires, so essential for cooking and heating, needed an insatiable amount of dry wood, and it fell to the children of all classes to scavenge for all they could find. Boys would haul branches to be chopped and stored, while small girls sought out armsful of kindling. While most forests belonged to the king or other powerful landowners, extracting wood from them was strictly regulated, with harsh penalties for infringement. Most of the peasants could acquire only that harvested by farm-workers' hook or shepherds' crook, in other words not by felling trees or chopping boughs. Æthelgifu's father fortunately owned the surrounding woodlands, so the royal fires were well provided.

She shook herself from the reverie of recollection, and asked Tild about some of the other people who had come to work within the new abbey enclosure.

"There's grumpy old Godwin, the chief cooper. His barrels are well-made, my father said, and he knows that because he helps old Aart, the smith, who makes the iron bands for them. Both my father and Aart shoe all the horses in the burh — and there's lots of them. But old Aart has two sons. One works with my father, as farrier, the other works with his, but making weapons and armour. They have two male slaves to help them. Grown-up ones of course. Franks in their case. Both so handsome! But of course, I wouldn't look at them! I'm answered for." The last was said with a wistful smile. Æthelgifu was intrigued.

"To whom?"

"Why to Alwyn, Master Chad's older son." Tild replied, blushing. "My father once saved the reeve's life, when they were both fighting Danes a while back. Just like my uncle, really. But instead of becoming a warrior — after all, my father had a job as farrier even then — he was offered his young son Alwyn to marry me."

"Do you want to?" asked Æthelgifu, and instantly regretted the intrusive question.

"Oh yes, my Lady. For he's a real good match and has a good heart. I love him lots, but I know he fancies Blaedswith, daughter of Oswald the baker. I fear he'll never be a loving, steady husband while she is there to take his eye."

Æthelgifu was alarmed that this child should be so preoccupied with thoughts of marriage, when she had not yet begun to be a woman. Although legally considered adult at aged ten, and able to inherit in their own right, yet the bodies of girls of that age were still immature. To take her mind off the subject, she asked Tild to take her to see the geese and their goslings, for which Tild had responsibility when she was not working for the abbess.

On their way through the enclosure from the Abbess House, they met Chad. He strode up and stood before them, thumbs tucked into his belt and legs apart. His trimmed grey beard showed up the redness of his fat face, and his thick lips seemed to sneer as he spoke.

"My Lady Abbess," he began, then gave a little laugh. "There are matters of law which need your attention, as soon as possible. As landowner over the estates given by your father and others to this abbey, you are entitled to sit in judgement on those who are accused of lawbreaking upon your land. Will you attend this afternoon's court session? You can delegate the role of judge to me, and I advise you to do so, seeing as you are so young and lacking experience in these matters."

The prioress had joined the group and stood behind Chad nodding her head in support of his suggestion, and pursing her lips.

"I think I had better not yet assume such a responsibility, Master Chad. While I am so new in my office it is better that I do not stand in judgement upon others. By all means represent me, and thank you, Sir."

The prioress smirked, and although Æthelgifu felt relieved of this onerous duty, yet there was a rising sense of being belittled by her previous superior. One day, she told herself, I shall have the courage both to defy Mistress Edith and to learn the laws. Just then, Chad turned to Tild.

"Tild, I wish to speak with you about your wedding with my Alwyn. Your father and I have agreed terms, and now we just need to arrange the date and details. With your permission, Madam."

Æthelgifu nodded her consent, and Chad drew Tild away by the arm. Æthelgifu was left facing Prioress Edith.

"Well, Abbess," said the older women. "You are wise not to take on too much so soon. But I do believe you should take more interest in the new intake of postulants. I have interviewed each one personally, and there are one or two among them who cause me some concern, young Hild for example. They do not seem to realise that they will be here for the whole of their lives. Their parents have paid generous dowries, and most have their own servants with them, but they must not be allowed to be idle. There is much to do."

"Indeed, Lady Edith. You are right. I shall attend to them at once."

"And spend less time with that servant-girl, perhaps."

Just when Æthelgifu was controlling her response to the prioress, that last remark, said as the woman turned her back and walked away, caused the abbess to clench her teeth and make fists of her hands. A slight hiss was all the sound she allowed herself.

CHAPTER 6

APPOINTMENTS

EACH DAY BEGAN TO SETTLE to a routine. Tild, sleeping on a straw pallet on the opposite side of the firepit from her mistress, woke first, just before dawn, to help her mistress prepare for Laud. She brought water for her to wash her face and hands and removed the chamber pot to dispose of its contents. She would hand over a small stick, dipped in salt, for Æthelgifu to clean her teeth, and a goblet of water to dilute the salt prior to spitting it out. On Sundays a clean linen undergarment would be exchanged for the one the abbess lived in for the week. Afterwards Tild would go to tend her geese and engage in general duties around the enclosure until the abbess needed her again.

After the Divine Office of Prime followed by Mass, being between half past seven and eight o'clock, the prioress joined the abbess in her house to break their fast with bread and cheese, and goblets of milk, warmed over the firepit. They discussed the matters of the day and distributed their responsibilities between them.

One morning Edith announced to Æthelgifu that she would appoint Wulfthrith as subprioress, her assistant. This was an older nun who had accompanied Edith when she had arrived in Shaftesbury to prepare for the community arriving from Wimborne. She looked at Æthelgifu with such a hard stare as she said this, that she dared not contradict. Yet Æthelgifu felt uncomfortable whenever Wulfthrith was around. The woman, conscious of her kinship with King Osbert of Northumbria, had a way of making Æthelgifu feel small, stupid and insignificant. She spoke with a sneer and heard her abbess's suggestions and opinions with a little laugh, as though amused by a silly puppy.

Æthelgifu's annoyance spurred her to make an appointment of her own, almost daring Edith to deny her.

"I have decided to appoint our Sister Tatswith, Tate, as Mistress of Guests. She has all the qualities to put people at their ease, and with her background as an educated woman brought up in the royal court, knows all the social graces."

"If you think so," replied the prioress with ill-concealed disapproval. "I always found her somewhat frivolous when she was at Wimborne. But you know her better — always together as you were." Æthelgifu was delighted at her small victory, and that her friend should have one of the most envied roles in the community.

After their conference, they joined the religious community in the Great Hall, just as the women's empty platters of bread or bowls of porridge had been cleared away. The servants then withdrew and the Handmaids and vowesses sat at the trestles in order, the ones holding offices nearest the High Table, other professed Handmaids beyond them and the novices furthest back. Postulants and lay persons were not allowed into this daily formal assembly.

The abbess sat in the centre of the High Table looking down the two rows of her Sisters. A lectern was placed before her, with a Bible in the English tongue, opened. Æthelgifu stood and read aloud a chapter, the one following the chapter read the day before. The first time she stood, her knees trembled. She hoped no-one would notice the slight shaking of her habit. They all did, of course, but made allowances and most felt empathy for the youngster. Wulfthrith nudged her neighbour, but that good lady failed to rise to her malice. Æthelgifu's voice at first sounded thin and reedy, and she pushed out the words in a rush. As the days passed her legs lost their wobble and the voice developed in strength and volume, and she learnt to pace the words and imbue them with sense and meaning.

After the reading she and the prioress informed the community of events, such as the expected arrival of guests or new pupils, or the need for extra workers in the infirmary following an outbreak of disease. The Handmaids were invited to make any reports they had prepared, or ask questions or seek guidance. The regular meeting, called a Chapter after the portion of daily reading, then moved into the section which most of them dreaded, especially the abbess. She remembered it well from her own days as a lowly nun, and even more now she had to bear an onerous responsibility.

The Chapter of Faults began with each professed Sister in turn either making a public confession or declaring 'Pass'. Æthelgifu could not remember a time when Mistress Wulfthrith did not pass.

The Handmaids' faults could be as trivial as entertaining an unkind thought about another Sister, or as grievous a sin as stealing an extra portion of food in the kitchen, or beating a slave for a fault without hearing an excuse. Sisters were invited to report on each other, ostensibly to avoid secret feuds or gossip. But mostly it pained the accused and, especially if considered unjust, produced rancour in her heart. But then, that would have to be confessed too. After each admission of fault, the abbess had to issue a penalty. This could range from a few prayers, to being obliged to perform unwelcome duties. Mostly Æthelgifu tried to make the penance enable the culprit to make up for her omission of charity by making her do something kind, or of obedience by making her realise the value of responsibility.

When two of the new intake of novices were accused by others of flirting with some of the young masons working within the enclosure, Æthelgifu banned them from conversing with any man other than Wilfric the mass-priest, who was married and would take no nonsense. She also gave the two young women the unpopular duty, usually the work of the slaves, of cleaning the latrine seats (the planks with cut-out holes erected over a pit), every day for a month and providing fresh, scented water and clean towels for hand washing. Seeing there were sufficient dockleaves for hygienic use was also part of that duty. The two young sisters, stricken with shame, accepted their penances with dutiful obedience, much to their abbess's relief.

After a few weeks, some of the young postulants were exhibiting homesickness, showing redness around their eyes and going into long reveries, forgetful of the tasks in hand. The first flush of religious enthusiasm had worn off and they were beginning to miss the freedom of their childhoods. Æthelgifu came upon one young woman sitting alone in the chapel, crying and sobbing.

"Hild, what is the matter? Why the tears?" asked Æthelgifu with real concern. This was the first emotional crisis she had had to deal with as the girl's ultimate superior. When first interviewed, this girl showed no lack of religious motivation. She was always first into the chapel and learned long Scripture passages by heart. Yet now Hild was reluctant to open her heart to her Superior. Æthelgifu patiently sat with her on a bench placed along the far wall. Eventually Hild spoke, quietly, as if deeply ashamed.

"Oh, my Lady Abbess, it's not that I don't like the life here. Since Father left me here I have met with kindness. It's just... Well, I hate to tell you this, but I have this yearning to be a mother. I see the babies of the churls and ache to have one of my own — a boy to see grow into a warrior and bring me honour. But here..."

"I know," responded Æthelgifu, thoughtfully picking her words. "We all feel this from time to time — especially when Wilfric's wife is so big with child, and looks so happy to be so. But while he is a mass-priest, and I've heard of several clergy in other places having wives and children, that is not something allowed to us. We cannot dedicate our lives to God as Handmaids and be mothers too."

She paused while thinking of all those vowesses, seven of them now, widows and mothers. They seemed to have the best of all worlds, and now enjoyed the security of abbey life. But then she remembered that the lot of a mother was not all joyful.

"Think of our older Sisters, the vowesses," she said quietly, adding, "They have known the grief of losing a husband and, most of them have had many babies and children too die in their arms."

Her own beloved older sister then came to mind.

"Why, my own sister Athelflad of Mercia, I heard from recently, had a terrible time in labour. The babe lives but the agony of giving birth, the sheer pain for hours on end, for her was unendurable."

"Did she not drink an infusion of Pennyroyal?" asked the innocent, wide-eyed to hear such intimate details of a royal princess.

"Oh yes, plenty. But, and this is secret, mind, she will now not let Lord Athelred, her husband, go near her again. Not in that way. No chance of further children; no sons. She swears she would sooner die in battle than on the birthing stool!"

Hild, a girl of about thirteen years, went silent at these words and dried her eyes and cheeks. She was about to enter the Novitiate and Æthelgifu knew the stress of such a commitment at such an age. She had appointed one of the Handmaids from Wimborne as Novice Mistress, Mistress Elswith, a pleasant, mature woman who limped painfully from a riding accident in her youth. But Elswith was not happy, inhibited in her role by the constant interference from both Prioress Edith and her deputy, Mistress Wulfthrith. The latter usurped the authority of the Novice Mistress by beating the novices and oblates for the most trivial offences, without even consulting Elswith.

The two monks who had attended Æthelgifu's consecration with their abbot, John, stayed on after he returned to Athelney Abbey with the royal party. At his behest the two were obliged to teach the Handmaids the art of manuscript writing and embellishing, skills at which they themselves excelled. These two monks, Pepin and Mark, were both Franks — foreigners, as were most of the Athelney community, there being too few Saxon men willing to commit to religious life.

Having spent much of their religious lives in Constantinople and Rome, where there were stronger degrees of gender separation in religious life, these two were less than content to be assigned to a women's community. They felt it was a waste of their time teaching Handmaids of the Lord the craft of preparing parchments and the art of calligraphy.

Spinning and weaving were women's work, they reckoned, not illuminating manuscripts and writing Latin.

The two went around with barely disguised sneers and found owing obedience to a teenaged abbess tested their tolerance to the limit. Pepin, a thin, stooped figure with a highly creased face, was particularly ill tempered. Mark, taller and angular, was rather more patient with his lot in life, and with the young women under his tutelage. But even he did not hesitate in offering criticism — wanted or not.

After a month at Shaftesbury, they applied for, and were granted, permission to be transferred back to Athelney. This religious community, the male counterpart to Shaftesbury Abbey but with no royal at its head, was just starting up its own school of writing and needed their expertise. Sighs of relief were heaved by all.

Sweterun, the young nun appointed to be cellarer — in charge of the provision of food and drink — soon found her responsibilities too much for her alone, especially when some of the community complained about the quality of the food. She asked for an assistant, but Prioress Edith had not yet discussed the choice of appointee with the abbess. When the time came, both leading women chose one of the older pensioners, a widow with experience of running a household. One by one the necessary offices were filled for the smooth running of the abbey, with most of the full complement of the fully professed religious women being given specific roles or work tasks. As numbers joined them and made their vows, more posts were distributed so no-one could be accused of idleness.

At the same time every day, except for Sundays and feast days, the monk Grimbald came to join the two Superiors to report on progress in the building plan. Occasionally he took the abbess aside to advise her on how to implement the Rule of St Benedict which he had observed as more strictly adhered to on the Continent than in Saxon lands. After a few times of his gentle chiding, Æthelgifu asked him to expound on the Rule, a little at a time, every day at the end of Mass. This he did, and did very well. There was some reluctance within the community, however, to implementing some of the restrictions in the Rule, such as adopting plain rough dress and not owning individual property. Most of the Handmaids had been accustomed to luxury and finery in their previous lives, being the daughters of ealdormen and the noblest thegns. Giving all that up as well as the chance of motherhood and of controlling households demanded of them a compensatory degree of religious enthusiasm to which not all were dedicated. Æthelgifu often found herself faced with sulkiness in a Sister or a flouting of the Rule that taxed her good judgement. Fortunately, her own sense of the rightness of the Benedictine Rule combined with common sense, good humour and amiability, usually restored the atmosphere within the community to one of general cheerfulness.

Master Asser, the Welsh monk who was a close confident and adviser to the king, remained at Shaftesbury for only a short time, but promised to return. On his brief first visit, he encouraged the whole community to attempt the study of Latin, leaving with them his servant, a gifted scholar from southern Italy called Matteo, to teach them. A hunchback with a sensitive face and neatly trimmed beard, his good humour and lack of pomposity endeared him to everyone. He made learning Latin an enjoyable undertaking, praising freely and encouraging even the dullest learner.

Children from the burh and nearby hamlets began to be enrolled in the house of learning, or school, alongside several child oblates of both sexes. One of the larger buildings near the entrance gate was designated for this role. Chosen to lead the teaching was young Mistress Wynflad. She was clever, learning quickly the Latin basics from Matteo, sufficient to begin instructing the children. Their chanting of declensions and conjugations could be heard over the din of the stonemasons and the usual enclosure sounds. Wynflad was a slight girl in her mid-teens, born with one eye constantly turned outward. From a wealthy family, she wore a silken underdress and more jewellery than strictly allowed. The band around her headdress was of finely worked silver, and she arrived at the abbey with two servants of her own. These were co-opted to help instil discipline in the classroom and to aid the slower learners. They were learning to read and write themselves and, but for coming from homes of well-off churls or lesser thegns rather than noble ealdormen, would have entered religious life themselves.

CHAPTER 7
ALWYN AND EDWIN

MOST AFTERNOONS, between Sext and None, when the Lord's Handmaids were employed in quiet pursuits such as private prayer or studying, Æthelgifu would meditate. In that first summer she often stood under a spreading tree at the top of the southern slope while admiring the view over the hills and valleys. The steep side of the hill below her was recently planted with apple trees and vines, with sheep allowed to graze the grasses and weeds between the rows. The following year they would be able to make their own wine and vinegar.

How bountiful is God, she reflected, and how wonderful is life in all its variety and complexity. Yet nature, she knew, could be cruel, with famines and savage animals a constant threat. While developing such thoughts one day, she saw a sad-faced Tild approach up the hillside with a basket of wild herbs and other useful plants on her arm.

"Why so sad, Tild?" she asked when the girl was near.

"Because Masters Alwyn and Edwin are being sent by their father to Tisbury, ten mile or so away, and they'll have to pass through dangerous forests before they get there. And you know what waits in forests to jump on Christian men, don't you?"

Æthelgifu looked nonplussed. "Why the dark elves, of course, my Lady. They do jump out at travellers and attack them. And they turn the wood spirits against them and make them drop their branches which frighten the horses and make the riders fall, and then the wild animals get them and... Oh, I'm so afraid for them. There are only two soldiers from the burh going with them."

"Oh Tild... Why are they going?"

"Because Master Chad wants them to investigate a crime committed there, that being one of the hides given to the abbey by your father, my Lady. Something about a young churl, a lad of twelve years but who's taken the frankpledge, and so is bound to keep the law and honour his lord. They say he spoke evil about your father the king, and his titheman confronted him about that and the lad struck him with a seax and wounded him bad-like."

"That's really serious," commented the King's

daughter, knowing that abusing a lord, in this case verbally attacking the King and physically his village superior, could be punished by death.

"It's only a rumour," said Tild, eyes welling up with compassion for the boy and his possible fate, "so Chad wants his sons to see what truth there is to it and bring the young accused lad back for trial – but only if it warrants it. They'll be going tomorrow at first light and should be back by nightfall. But see here, my Lady, I have an amulet I'm going to give Master Alwyn, to wear around his neck. This should keep him safe."

She drew out a small pouch on a cord from the basket, extracted an object from it and displayed it proudly on the palm of her hand. Æthelgifu studied it intently — a circular stone formed of a segmented spiral, like a curled worm, narrower in the middle and growing wider as it grew to the edge. She picked it up and felt the cold stone, turning it all ways, before returning it to Tild's hand with a sense of unease.

"It is well carved, but where did you acquire this?"

"Why, from a soldier who had found it at the coast. He says there be lots and lots like that down there on the beach, hidden within stones — carved by the sea spirits. Anyway, they work powerfully against elvish tricks and curses. So I'm giving it to Alwyn, along with some particular herbs, in this little pouch for him to wear as he goes along. That sets my mind at rest, somewhat."

Thoroughly disturbed, Æthelgifu thought hard about the implications of Tild's speech, and her belief in the effectiveness of the curious shell-like stone. That evening, she asked Tild to come to her house after her dinner chores in the Great Hall, after Vespers but before Compline. When the serving-girl arrived, a little nervous at the formal manner of her summons, she found Æthelgifu in a serious frame of mind.

"I am troubled, Tild," said the young abbess, "at your belief in the old pagan ways. I daresay your parents and grandparents told you those tales of elves and wood spirits. But you are supposed to be a Christian now, and cast such thoughts behind you. So look, I have here a little carved cross — like the one Our Saviour died upon so many years ago. I want you to take this and throw that stone shell away, or better still, bury it. This cross will protect you and anyone from all evil spirits — spirits sent by the Devil to try to spoil God's work. Put this in the pouch and give this to Alwyn. Will you?"

The girl began to cry. It was a lot to take in and she was confused. She so wanted her kind young mistress to approve of her, and she really was a Christian, or so she thought. But how could she give up the beliefs of her ancestors, her people — beliefs they had held from the days before they came to this land? She took the cross, amid many thank-yous and sobs, and ran out of the abbess's house to think it all through.

Æthelgifu also left, but to go to see the prioress. She had been reluctant to share Tild's account, told to her almost in confidence. But an older head was now required.

"I'm not surprised," was Edith's response. "Only yesterday I had to beat the slave Skadi when I found votive food offerings hidden around my quarters. When I confronted her about it, she defiantly asserted they were for the Nissers, those elvish creatures that Vikings believe in, that demand amounts of tiny food and clothing offerings. In my house! I wasn't having that! So I beat her soundly and told her not to bring her pagan Danish notions into this Christian abbey."

"Was she upset?"

"Oh indeed, cried like a stuck pig, though whether that was from the pain of the thrashing or remorse at her wicked ways, I don't know. Mind you, that coiled creature in stone that Tild had — they do say that Abbess Hild, she the head of Whitby Abbey of two centuries or so back, once found so many snakes that she cut their heads off and threw them in the sea, where they turned into stone. But they're from the Devil, obviously, so Tild shouldn't be thinking they can protect anyone from elves. Only prayers can do that."

Æthelgifu left, unsure whether deepseated pagan traditions and beliefs could be removed from minds by beatings rather than conversion. She was also confused about whether elves really existed at all, as she could remember no mention of them in any of the Scripture she had read. More material for her periods of contemplation and study, obviously.

On her way to her quarters, she decided to seek out the slave Skadi. Her pagan ways intrigued her and the fact she had held onto them for so many years despite living among Christians. She called in to the various service buildings, the kitchen, the bakery, the brewery, and found her just outside the smithy, helping the blacksmith build up piles of logs to feed the furnace. She called her aside for 'a quiet word'. The girl dropped her logs and crept forward with little steps, shaking and with the pupils of her grey eyes dilated with fear.

"Oh, don't worry, Skadi," chided the abbess gently, smiling to reassure her. "I'm not going to punish you. Mother Edith has done so enough, I hear. No, come, sit here." She indicated the bench against the wall of the smithy, where the smith was accustomed to take his rests in the cooler air than in his workplace inferno. Æthelgifu, the royal princess, sat at one end and the Viking slave girl at the other.

"Tell me about yourself," asked Æthelgifu. "Where are you from, and who are your parents?"

Skadi froze, unable to believe that anyone, let alone the greatest Lady, should be taking a personal interest in her. For long she had considered herself to be as all the world told her she was, the lowest of human kind, not much more important than an animal. She existed to serve, that is all. Now, she is to talk about herself? She studied the face of her questioner. Was this a trick? Would she be flogged for saying something this Head Handmaid would find offensive? But Æthelgifu remained calm, gently smiling with both lips and eyes. Surely here was no oppressor!

Skadi swallowed hard and after spluttering a sound, unused to speaking, cleared her throat, and began,

"My mother was a Slav from a village on the River Dnieper, near Kyivan Rus, far to the East. The Varangians, you call them Vikings, came as traders between their northern lands and Byzantium, and captured her along with her family and many others. She was made a slave and taken to Sweden, where she was bought by a Danish warrior. He was my father, Hakon. His father was a farmer but, with six sons, there was little land for Hakon, one of the youngest. So he and my mother came here to the Danelaw land in eastern England. They settled here and farmed and had two children. I was the first. My little sister died just after she was born. That was really sad."

She paused, and looked up to see if what she was saying was accepted. The account was so detailed and pat, it had obviously been taught to her by her mother. She cherished it as her only inheritance, rehearsing it to herself to remember she had an identity, of sorts.

Æthelgifu nodded, "Go on!"

"Well, a few years ago, after a really bad harvest, father and the men from the village thought they could get better land if they came further West. They fought with Saxons and ..." Now she knew she was treading on thin ice.

Æthelgifu said simply "And?"

So she continued. "The Saxons were too strong for them, more and more came to defend their own farmers. My father and most of the men were killed. Some managed to escape back to their homes but the Saxons came looking for them. When they came to our village they killed all the men in it, even young boys and old men, and some of the women too. My mother and I were taken prisoner by one of King Alfred's thegns and we were sent to Winchester to work for him there. I was so young I don't really know what happened, but remember being brought here on horseback to the burh. Three of us small children were on one horse, and it made some of the Saxons laugh to see us holding each other as the horse was drawn on a leading rope behind one of the warriors. We three were always together until I was brought here just before you arrived, my Lady."

"How do you remember your pagan ways?"

"I don't really. Just some of the stories we were told as little children. The three of us slave-children told each other the ones we remember from our Viking days. My mother said that there were some Christians among the Slavs when she was young, followers of someone called Cyril. And there was another man, Methodius, who made many of her people Christian. But all her people were killed or enslaved by Vikings like my father."

"Is it true that some slaves of Vikings are killed, sacrificed, when their masters die?"

"My mother told me that she had heard of that but did not know if it was true. My father was not like that. He loved my mother and did not consider her a slave."

"Nevertheless, you know that we Christians never do such terrible things. We treat our slaves well, do we not? Have you any complaints?"

"Oh no, my Lady!" asserted Skadi. "Very well, my Lady! No complaints, no!"

Æthelgifu understood the reason for such vehemence. "Listen," she said confidingly, "if you do, if you feel wronged or unjustly treated any time, by anyone, you just come to me. Understood? By anyone. Now go and continue your work. And thank you for being honest with me and answering my questions."

The girl made off quickly, blushing deeply and with pounding heart. Æthelgifu remained for a moment, thinking. Then the bell went for the next Office.

Early the next morning Chad bade his two sons farewell before they were to ride off in the company of two of the soldiers from the burh. Wilfric, the mass-priest pronounced a blessing on them all, and the four men bowed in acknowledgement. Then they clattered off over the cobbles, with Tild giving her beloved Alwyn a shy wave and receiving a grin and a wink in return. Æthelgifu, watching from the chapel door as she was about to enter for the second of the daily Offices, whispered her hope that God would be with them on their way. All afternoon Tild kept her eyes on the great entrance and sometimes ventured onto Bimport to see if the party was returning. By nightfall, even Æthelgifu was concerned and sent for Chad to ask if he had received word.

"Oh, my Lady Abbess, no, I have not and I confess I am beginning to worry. They should have returned by now — even if they had stopped for something to eat on the way. The thegn Cynehelm has promised to send out a search-party from the burh if they do not return by sun-up. Thank you for your concern, my Lady, and please continue to pray for my lads."

He left the abbess's lodgings more agitated, more human and humble, she thought, than she had ever seen him. She tried to stop her imagination from picturing the various dangerous traps the young men might have fallen in — from robbers and wild-animal attacks to the seductions of pretty country women. The thought of the last caused her to shudder for poor Tild's peace of mind.

At dawn the next day, the men still not having returned, an armed cohort set off from the burh to look for them. Tild was shaking with anxiety, having not slept a moment in the night. She and Æthelgifu heard the soldiers riding along Bimport, and an hour or two later, riding back towards the entry-gate to the abbey. The two women, along with several others and led by Chad, rushed out of their buildings towards the approaching party.

What they saw filled them with horror.

Two men, Edwin and one of the soldiers, were bloodied and filthy, leading their horses, each with a body secured over its back. Alwyn and the other soldier were dead, dried blood and black bruises obscuring their faces and heavily soiling their ripped clothing. Tild's scream when she beheld her intended husband chilled to the bone all who heard it. The two wounded survivors were gently lowered from their horses and carried by servants into the Great Hall, where they were laid beside the fire. Other servants, led by Chad, attended to the two dead men, carrying them into one of the huts to prepare their bodies for burial. Two of the vowesses and their own two servants were deputed to see to that sad task.

Meanwhile the Sister Infirmarian got to work on the invalids, ordering bowls of clean warm water and towels as she and her lay assistant stripped the men of their bloodied garments. This Sister Infirmarian was one of the older women, a widow whose own sons had been slain, and who had entered religious life on becoming widowed. She gently washed the wounds and called for poultices of healing herbs to be fetched. On receiving and applying them to the wounds, she then bandaged them and covered both patients in blankets, as they were shivering, despite lying near to the flames.

Chad and Cynehelm arrived and Æthelgifu allowed them to approach the wounded men, but only so long as Sister Infirmarian approved. The distraught reeve asked his surviving son what had happened.

"We were on our way back from Tisbury, where

we heard the evidence and witnesses, but dropped the case..."

"Yes, yes. Never mind that — what happened to you?"

"Well, we followed the path through the woods and came to a clearing with a pond. We dismounted to let the horses rest a while and drink from the pond when we noticed a fire had been lit nearby, the ashes still red with heat. We were afraid, I can tell you. Suddenly, from behind the trees around us a group of Danes leapt out. We didn't stand a chance!"

"The heathen bastards!"

"There were more of them than us, but the four of us fought them hard. We managed to kill three or four of them and the others ran away. That's when we realised Alwyn was badly wounded, as was Sven who was one of our guards. He was still standing, axe in hand, but blood was pouring out of his other arm and from a gash in his neck. We managed to get him on his horse, and had to sling Alwyn across the back of his, tied with cord to stop him falling off. Oh father, it was terrible. Those Danes were battle-hardened warriors and we were taken by surprise!"

Chad was overcome on hearing this. His face reddened and tears streamed down it. He patted Edwin's shoulder, told him how proud he was of him, then he spoke as though he were being strangled but forcing out the words,

"My son, my Alwyn, he died a warrior's death. There is no greater honour. I'll see that he and Sven receive every acknowledgement of their bravery."

With that, he left the hall – unwilling to let the women see his grief.

Sven was buried in full military honours in the burh. His fellow soldiers held a collection and gained several shillings which they presented to his widow. Her neighbours vowed to support her and her young children and, with all that and the King's pension, the bereft woman found some comfort.

Alwyn was buried next to the church, the first of many such inhumations. The hole was measured to accommodate the five feet eight inches of the corpse, the normal size of a Saxon man. Wrapped in a white shroud, with his feet facing East so that when he rose again he would be facing Jerusalem and the Returned Christ, he was lowered onto a straw pallet by leather bands which were withdrawn once the body was settled. The Bishop of Sherborne led the prayers, while the Handmaids stood around, respectfully giving front place to the family – the wounded Edwin, supported on crutches, and the grieving father. Tild, next to Chad, was weeping noisily, comforted by her friend, the slave Skadi.

Chad the Reeve suddenly held aloft a spear and shield that had belonged to Alwyn. Why he had brought them was now made clear.

"Bishop, I ask, nay plead," he said with a cracked voice, "that these be placed alongside my son – as our warrior forefathers would have done in days gone by."

He began to lower them towards the open grave when Bishop Wulsige's voice rang out with all the force of a younger man, "Stop! No, I forbid it. These things were done before we believed in the Christian faith. Your son will not need them in heaven. It is not Valhalla! Whether your son is judged now or at the Judgement Day we do not rightly know – but we do know that weapons, jewellery and all that sort of thing will not be needed there! Amen."

With that he turned and stormed off, red-faced and shaking with anger. Chad dropped to his knees, the spear and shield clattering as they were tossed aside. There, in the mud beside his elder son's mortal remains, he wept, sobbing more loudly than Tild, who quickly knelt alongside him, putting her arm around his back to comfort him. Edwin looked stricken and required two of the nearest Handmaids to support his frame as he hobbled back with them to the infirmarium.

As days went by, Edwin grew stronger and returned almost to full vigour. But Tild was not the same as she had been. Sorrow aged her and slowed down her movements. More than once she begged the abbess to let her take vows and be a virgin for ever. Æthelgifu was sorry she could not allow her, for the Religious at Shaftesbury, as in most other places, were all from the top class of nobility – daughters or widows of ealdormen or noble warriors, not of tradesmen, churls or freedmen. But she promised that Tild would be her own chief personal servant for as long as she wished, and gave permission for her to attend all the Offices and Masses of the Sisters. She asked her also to recruit an assistant from among the freeborn girls in the burh – as most royal women, abbesses or not, had several servants to attend them, and Æthelgifu was feeling more confident in her role as leading personage in the community.

CHAPTER 8

THE HOLY CROSS MYSTERY

THREE DAYS AFTER ALWYN'S burial, Æthelgifu asked Chad if he would produce the relic of the Holy Cross for displaying on the altar the following day, Good Friday. To see, however obscured or tiny, a portion of the True Cross upon which the Saviour died, on the anniversary of that momentous death would be a wonderful experience, leading the worshippers into deeper belief and reverence.

"By all means, my Lady. I have it locked away in a safe place. It is within that splendid casket your father so generously bestowed upon us. Allow me some moments to retrieve it and I'll send for Wilfric to bring it to the chapel. It is only right that a priest should carry the precious relic. We'll meet you there shortly."

Æthelgifu nodded and made her way to the

chapel to await the arrival of the precious relic. While waiting there she opened a page of the massive Bible upon the lectern, and was translating some of the Latin verses when, suddenly, shouting and the sound of running footsteps drew away her attention. The reeve and the mass-priest burst into the chapel, panting hard and with eyes wide.

The two men blurted out, shouting in panic:

"Oh Mother Abbess!"

"Oh noble lady!"

"It's gone, quite gone!"

"It's gone, my Lady – stolen away!"

Wilfric crossed himself: Chad pulled off his cap and clutched it, knuckles showing white in his beefy hands.

"What do you mean, it's gone?" asked Æthelgifu, with sinking heart. "The reliquary?"

"Yes, good ma'am," stammered Chad, "the Holy Relic in its reliquary is not in the casket. It's not there!"

After a few moments the men collected themselves, Æthelgifu having suggested they sat on the wall-bench while they recovered. Wilfric prayed something repetitive under his breath while Chad took several deep breaths. He then explained.

"Well, Abbess, after your father gave the casket into my safekeeping, I looked inside and saw the loveliest, the most finely worked gold artefact I ever did see, containing that which is most precious in the world. You saw how wonderful was the casket? Well, the reliquary is even finer, but smaller, much smaller..."

"Yes, yes," chided Æthelgifu impatiently, "but what has happened to it?"

"Well, when I went to take the casket, all wrapped up in finest cloth as it was, from the strong chest where I had laid it, locked with this stout key..."

"Yes?"

"I took out the casket — it looked like no-one had touched it since I placed it there — but when I opened it — it was empty. There was only the wool padding covered in fine silk on which it rested. But no reliquary — no True Cross."

Chad fell to his knees, as anguished about this as when he found Alwyn had died, and then when he was thwarted from burying his warrior weapons with him. So many blows in such a short time. He squatted and sobbed. Wilfric continued his prayers, and Æthelgifu wondered what on Earth she was to do.

She decided to leave the priest and the reeve to seek the advice of Prioress Edith. That lady's immediately response was stunned silence. She had to sit down to recover herself. After receiving a restorative draught of wine thoughtfully administered by the abbess, she then began to accuse almost everyone who had visited the abbey since

Æthelgifu's consecration. Her most severe denunciation was of the honesty of the abbey's slaves.

"These heathen slaves, the Danes. They worship trees, wood. I expect, I almost know, that one of them took it, prompted by the Devil. I'll kill them! They'll burn in hell!"

Æthelgifu, alarmed at the vehemence of Edith's speech and the high colour of her face sought to lighten the atmosphere by saying, with the hint of a laugh,

"When they find it won't work miracles for them — free them from their bondage, perhaps, they'll give it back."

Edith tutted, thought for a moment, then replied, "Our simple people too still cling to the belief in tree-elves and forest-elves. That these wicked elves who do such harm to people could be placated by this piece of the holiest of trees! Wicked nonsense. They would think that. Any of them could have stolen it!"

Æthelgifu was plunged into instant despair. Even her good humour could not save her. The thought of such paganism and treachery in her own abbey territory where she had thought to bring only goodness and light, depressed her beyond words.

Edith, somewhat calmer, was about to condemn all the laypeople round about, when she stopped herself in order to be more constructive.

"Now listen, think. Let's not spoil the Triduum —

after all, they're the three holiest days of the year – by discussing it further."

Æthelgifu nodded, too stunned to speak. Edith continued with quiet determination.

"Say nothing to anyone about this. I'll have words with Master Chad and the priest. They must tell no-one. It would bring disgrace and shame upon us all."

Edith's spelling out the implications and likely repercussions of this great loss increased the weight in Æthelgifu's stomach. Her eyes smarted as she watched the prioress's swift departure. To her mind were conjured dreadful scenes of a royal visitation with shire reeves and ealdormen, bishops and abbots, accusing her and her abbey of negligence in allowing such a treasure to be stolen. Her beloved father could accuse her of blasphemy by treating the precious papal gift so lightly that it could be stolen. Slaves and servants would face trials and be hanged, if not worse. Her friend Tild, tortured? Chad too, no doubt.

She had to sit where Edith had been seated. The goblet and wine jug were within reach, so she poured some and gulped it down.

What will become of me? She dreaded the answer. At the least she would be expelled and sent to a remote convent, cold and merely basic. Forgotten and neglected. Oh, St Cuthburga and all the Saxon Saints! Come to our aid! Tears began to flow and her whole body trembled.

Calm down, breathe deeply. Trust in God's Providence. With the help of heaven — oh sweet Mary! — the whole matter would be resolved before anyone knew of the theft of the sacred object. Please, God.

Silence and secrecy were now, as Edith said, essential.

Sombre Good Friday was spent in fasting and meditation, with no mention of the relic of the Holy Cross despite so much of the liturgy centring on that original obscene instrument of Roman execution reserved specifically for slaves and rebels.

Then the joyful Easter feast came and went. The heightened midnight ceremonies were celebrated in happy spirit by most of the community — while a small group, the people of greatest responsibility, felt nothing beneath their smiles but a sickening dread. The theft of the Holy Cross soured everything.

After the morning Mass the community, including the lay workers and household servants, feasted and drank the good quality wine saved for the special occasion. To the members of the small group, nothing tasted other than bitter or bland. Everyone else enjoyed themselves, filling their stomachs after the Lenten fast. Even the slaves had the means to buy extra food and comforts from selling goods, mostly gifts or things earned in their spare time, at their markets during the Wednesday of the Ember Days in Lent.

On Easter Sunday night, the soldiers in the burh made such a noise — loud drunken singing and laughter — that Chad was sent to request their silence to enable the abbey community to sleep. Loud guffaws. and shouted profanities greeted his request, but the noise did soon abate. Not that Æthelgifu was afforded much sleep. Keeping her secret from Tild was an extra cause of anxiety. The younger girl's common sense would have been a welcome antidote. But was she herself the culprit? Did she know who was?

The days of Eastertide passed with no further news of the theft of the reliquary, nor was there any further sighting or threat from the Danish gang that had attacked Alwyn.

Peace and silence should have reigned.

The abbey enclosure however was far from being a quiet and contemplative place. Building work on the stone church proceeded with much hammering, sawing, chiselling and other noise. Dozens of churls and slaves had been drafted in from the burh and settlements around to prepare ground for the building project. Nobody ever communicated other than by shouting.

Overseen by Master Grimbald and chivvied along by Chad, the labourers constructed scaffolds and crane-devices from tree trunks. Quarrymen dug out the greensand nearby from the hillside itself and a chain of ox-carts drew rough-hewn stone up the pitiless slope. The carts were emptied onto stone-working ground just east of the perimeter of the enclosure. Here the masons, covered in grey stone-dust, hammered and chiselled until the blocks met the requisite dimensions. A gateway in the eastern palisade wall was created to enable the heavy masonry to be brought in on horse-drawn carts. While most of the stone-dust gusted eastwards in clouds away from the abbey, occasionally the wind changed, and the dust blew over the enclosure, causing outbreaks of coughing and swearing from the workfolk there.

The hens, geese and goats continued to roam happily between the wooden huts, but were chased away impatiently by the masons and labourers as the stone building began to take shape.

Among the visitors to the abbey was one young man, already an ealdormen as his father had died recently and he had inherited vast tracts of land. Beornwulf was a Mercian, and his father had been one of the Lords of the Mercians. As a serious man of intelligence this father had been a close adviser to Æthelgifu's royal brother-in-law, Lord Ethelred.

When her older sister Athelflad was sent to marry the Mercian Lord, Alfred had demanded the young Beornwulf be brought into his Wessex court at Winchester as a sort of pledge of goodwill between the two people, or as a hostage in case anything bad happened to Athelflad at Mercian hands.

Tall, clean-shaven and with light brown wavy hair falling to his shoulders, he was handsome in a rather fine and delicate-looking way, a far cry from the usual beefy warriors with their bulging muscles, broad shoulders and moustaches grown long at their edges. The first time he rode into the grounds, Æthelgifu was spellbound.

"Oh, by Jesus, he looks so handsome!" she exclaimed out loud, then looked around to see if anyone had heard.

On his frequent visits, usually breaking his journey between Winchester and Alfred's new castle at Cheddar, he always carried letters or documents or gifts from the royal parents to their beloved second daughter and her abbey. Each time Æthelgifu's pleasure at seeing him increased. Not just for what he brought, but for his company. He was always respectful and polite, but there was a look of his which suggested he was thinking, weighing her up, approving. He and Æthelgifu shared similar tastes in poetry and song, and his knowledge of the people in court circles enabled her to feel close to her family.

On one occasion, Tild approached and he broke from the conversation to appraise the girl's body, his satisfied smile bringing a blush to the servant's cheeks and delivering a sharp pang of annoyance in her mistress.

When May came, and the Feast of the Finding of the Holy Cross on the third of the month, abbess, prioress, reeve and mass-priest held their collective breath lest the subject of their own portion of that cross were mentioned. Fortunately, if it was, they did not hear of it. But their sleep would often be invaded by nightmares – all connected in some way with the loss of the holy relic. They prayed that by the time of the Feast of the Exaltation of the Cross, in September, it might have reappeared. It did not.

One night, Æthelgifu lay wide awake, listening to the foxes bark and the owls hoot. She tossed and turned, cursing the ropes below her stuffed wool mattress. They had stretched in time under her weight and needed tightening to afford a more comfortable base. In the light of the embers in the fire-pit, she could see Tild the other side, lying on her palliasse and breathing slowly, snoring quietly.

That poor girl, bereaved of her betrothed, Æthelgifu mused. What must it be like to have heart-love for someone, an ordinary man, and have his heart-love for her? Does it involve a feeling, a warmth arising from below the stomach up to the face, causing it to blush? She has felt such an emotion, but with an accompanying sense of shame. Or is what Tild felt just a realisation, just a mind-love, that Alwyn would have been a good provider, a strong father of sturdy children? Was she to him just a potentially healthy mother for his children?

Yet she had been happy when she was with him, and he with her. There must have been feeling there. But is that feeling, the surging emotion, sinful in itself, something a Religious should never allow herself? The Church allows married people this, surely? There is nothing she had read in Scripture that says women have these feelings, only some men — like King David's heart-love for Bathsheba. But that was a wicked love as Bathsheba was already married. So some love can be good, like that St Paul says a husband should have for his wife. Æthelgifu's own mother and father love each other, of that she is sure. But is it to do with this feeling, or does that love become real only after years of sharing lives together? Is the feeling wrong in itself or is it only so depending on the person who provokes it? Obviously, if the feeling is for someone already betrothed or, worse, married to another, indulging that feeling, she knows from Church teaching, would be a great sin.

Æthelgifu found her mind seeking out great female saints to see if any among them demonstrated sinless love for a man. Yet none could she remember.

Most were virgins, or adopted chastity in or after marriage, or martyrs having protected their chastity to the point of death. Even Jesus's mother was a virgin. It was too complicated.

Æthelgifu found herself weeping. Her tears wetted her cheeks and she struggled not to sound out loud her sudden gulps and sobs. But, despite her efforts, Tild awoke and left her bed to comfort her mistress.

"No, Tild, it is you who needs my comfort," said Æthelgifu, sitting up and gently enfolding her young servant in her arms.

She looked at the young girl's upturned face, also now wet with tears. She held her more closely, kissing the top of the servant's head and letting her cry freely. After a time, the younger girl drew away, wiping her cheeks dry with the sleeve of her nightdress. Just as she was starting to apologise, Æthelgifu spoke over her.

"No, Tild. Listen! I have been holding back from you something that has been worrying me for some time." She then related the shameful account of the theft of the relic of the Holy Cross. She expected Tild to express horror but was relieved when the girl simply commiserated.

"This don't be your fault, my Lady — it's them that stole it is to blame. So don't be upset, my Lady. I know you've not been sleeping these past nights, but now I know what's kept you awake and afeared. So now you've told me, I can share your sorrow for it, so you can sleep soundly, while I will lie awake and do your worrying for you."

Æthelgifu almost laughed at the simple goodness of her dear young servant — no, friend, she corrected herself. She sent her back to her side of the firepit, while she snuggled back down under the blankets and soon fell asleep. Tild lay awake, trying to work out who could have made off with the sacred treasure.

As weeks and months went by, the grain in the fields ripened and the herb garden flourished: life followed its pattern with little interruption. Towards Autumn, the building of the church neared completion, with sturdy stone walls and a thickly thatched roof. Master Grimbald produced plans for the construction of further stone buildings and both abbess and prioress looked forward to the growing community having dormitories and a cloister.

More teenaged girls from noble families were arriving to be postulants almost weekly, and their dowries contributed to the increasing wealth of the abbey. Two widows presented themselves, one wished to take vows, and approached the abbess with zealous hope to be admitted. Her husband had succumbed to a wasting illness and she had spent several years tending him until she regarded his death as a relief, thanking God for it. Now she wished to spend the rest of her life praying for his soul, that it should be released from Purgatory and find its place in the Heavenly Realm.

The other woman, in her late forties, came with a sour face and truculent manner. She had been reluctant to leave her comfortable home, but her two sons had obliged her to do so, prompted by their wives, her daughters-in-law. They allowed her a handsome sum to cover accommodation and all expenses. Æthelgifu and Edith discussed long into the night whether or not to admit this elderly woman, as one strong personality with a grudge or over-critical nature can negatively impact the whole community. However, the large donation and the woman's great skill in needlework. — she had brought examples of her work with her — persuaded them to take the risk. Usually widows and other such pensioners contributed more than just money or land. They were happy to help in whatever way they could, allowing for creaking joints and painful arthritis. Some had real expertise in concocting herbal remedies and experience in dealing with the sick. Without the time-consuming obligation to attend all the Divine Offices during the day and night, they had more opportunity to tend those more elderly than themselves or see to the tradesmen and visitors while the Handmaids were at prayer.

Once the postulants had learnt something of the religious life, and proved themselves to be serious and industrious, they were admitted to the novitiate. As novices they wore simpler clothes, renounced worldly goods and swore to be obedient. In a year or two they would take their final vows and commit themselves forever to the House which they entered.

Young Mistress Gifu was in charge of the child oblates, now numbering five, as well as the new postulants, despite being not much older herself. But she had been a close friend of Æthelgifu in Wimborne, and always impressed her with her devotion to God coupled with a lively sense of fun and wonder. The younger women adored her, and tried to emulate her accomplishments and attitude. Her undoubted beauty and grace were unspoken about but enchanted almost all with whom she came into contact. She had rather less appeal to some of the older women.

When the church was completed, a Mass of dedication was conducted, with the elderly and ailing Bishop of Sherborne presiding and several local dignitaries attending. Holy water was sprinkled throughout the building, on walls and then the altar, and a small wooden box containing the fragmentary relics of the local Saxon St Juthwara placed in the chiselled-out hollow on the top of the altar stone. This was then sealed in by the bishop with freshly mixed mortar, and the altar washed with holy water. The King sent a letter of congratulations, along with the promise of a splendid new Sacramentary to be sent with Asser, to provide the mass-priest with the words to use in the liturgies. To Æthelgifu's huge relief, no mention was made of the Holy Cross relic which would have graced the newly dedicated church and altar with its greatest treasure. Nobody attending had heard much about the virgin-martyr St Juthwara, other than she was from Dorset, had been saintly, and thus suitable within the altar of a House of Holy Women. Even so, the clergy from Sherborne considered that, were they to have her remains, they could develop a decent cult for pilgrims around them. They would have to wait a few years for that.

The new church consisted of a simple rectangle comprising chancel and nave, with small high round-topped glazed windows and a sturdy wooden door with carved stone lintel and other embellishments. The frail and elderly could find repose upon the benches running along three sides of the wall. In front of the altar stood two reading desks, with tall carved candlesticks next to them. A scooped-out stone, jutting from the wall by the entrance held a small bowl of holy water, but there was no font, as this was the church for nuns alone. The people of the burh to the west and the growing settlement to the east of the abbey, had their own places of worship, small wooden and thatched churches served by the abbey's mass-priest.

The former chapel became an extra guest house for visiting clergy and monks, relieving the mass-priest and his wife from having to host them. They were occupied enough with their sickly newborn baby and a noisy active toddler.

CHAPTER 9
SCANDAL AVERTED

THE DAY AFTER THE DEDICATION ceremony of the new church was warm and sunny, the fifth in succession. Summer was yet to be on the wane. Æthelgifu walked to the top of the southern slope and, seeing human activity below her, made her way cautiously downwards. After almost slipping on the steep stony path, she stopped to catch her breath, and noticed a sleepy snake curled up in the long grass beside the track. Quickening her pace away from it, she arrived at an open gate in the wooden defensive fence. At the same time, another young woman was about to enter through it to climb up to the abbey. She was carrying a large hessian bag, an obvious heavy weight, on her back with a strap over her shoulder. She made way for the abbess to pass. Æthelgifu smiled in acknowledgement and warned her about the snake. Then she asked what was her load.

"Linen, madam. Dry now. Just gathered it off the bushes. I come down yesterday and washed it in the stream over there, though there's not so much water in it these hot days."

Æthelgifu let her pass and wandered over the field in the direction of the washer-woman's pointed finger. There were several women kneeling, intent on some activity, on either side of a small stream and singing together quietly, a repetitive chant. As she approached, they went quiet and stopped their work.

"Please don't stop," she said, curious to see what it was they were doing. Some were tending a large clay pot over a fire, with several smaller pots and piles of skeins of wool gathered around them. Others drew water from the stream in leather buckets. They nervously whispered to each other at the abbess's approach, watching her warily.

"What is it you are doing?"

"Why, we be dyeing, my Lady," spoke the boldest of them. "In this pot of boiling water we be changing the wool from sheep colour. See these?"

She pointed to skeins of wool of different hues, some blue, some brown and others yellow and gold.

"How do you do that?" asked Æthelgifu, who had always taken for granted the coloured skeins of wool spun and woven by women in all walks of life. Had she remained in Wimborne, she would have learnt those skills.

"Why, with certain plants, my Lady. Like these onion skins, and those black walnut hulls. And over there are sacks of marigold heads and golden rod."

Æthelgifu was intrigued. "These oak galls, and those twigs? Do they make colours?"

The women stifled laughter, fearful of causing offence but delighted to be superior in knowledge of these old skills to the royal young abbess. "Well, yes, but they also help the colours to take, like what's in that pot yonder."

Æthelgifu stepped to the indicated pot, lifted the lid and instantly recoiled with a loud and horrified "Urgh!" at the noxious stench released. It was worse than ten latrine pits. Now the women could not repress their mirth, holding their sides as they squatted among the heaps and pots. Some lost their balance and rolled, red faced with laughter, on the grass.

The abbess decided that smiling indulgently was the proper response, as no one had told her to lift the lid, after all.

"Why, Mother Abbess, that be fermented piss! That's why it stinks so. We use it with the woad plant to make a good blue dye, ma'am. I"m sorry you had to smell it. It takes a bit of getting used to."

"I'm sure it does," replied Æthelgifu with as much dignity as she could muster.

Another of the women gained the courage to speak, "Well, my Lady, if you think that be bad, don't go further downstream – or you may throw up all your food! The tanners be down there, around that hillside, and they use great quantities of stale piss for curing the leather. You can tell you're getting near them from the really awful stink."

"Aye, and the men smell rotten themselves, even after soaking theirselves in water!"

More gales of laughter followed that observation, and Æthelgifu thought it time to leave the group, so with a friendly nod of the head she left. She heard them still enjoying themselves as she climbed back up the stony path.

One day Brother Asser arrived from the Winchester court, accompanied by the handsome Mercian, Lord Beornwulf. The monk was to stay for a few weeks while the young nobleman was there only for sufficient time to rest his horse and collect some medicinal remedies for conveying to Cheddar, where several of the older ealdormen were suffering from elf-shot. Their bones were aching at the joints, as if elves had stabbed them.

In the abbess's house, Æthelgifu and Asser were soon deep in conversation over the beautifully decorated Sacramentary the monk had brought from Winchester, the gift promised by her father.

"This is known as the Gregorian Sacramentary," Asser explained. "This one book contains the words for all the services for the feasts of the saints, the seasons of the years, and the Sunday Masses too."

"So the three volumes of the Gelasian can be replaced by this one alone?"

"Indeed, my Lady. This has been used for a hundred years in the Carolingian Empire, ever since Pope Hadrian provided Charlemagne with this one authentic Roman Sacramentary. The Gelasian is good enough, but it is a mixture of traditions and really rather out of date. I'm sure your mass-priest will be pleased to use this new one."

Just then, a scuffling outside the door caused them to look up. Prioress Edith strode in, dragging with her by the arm a reluctant and distraught Sister Tate, Guest Mistress, the first appointment made by the abbess.

"This Sister," spat out Edith, "this disgrace to the abbey, has been seen – you tell them, girl. Go on, own up!"

Tate could hardly breathe, let alone speak. She hung her head and tears flowed down her cheeks and dripped off her chin. "I...I...can't!"

"No, because this wicked woman was found in the act of seducing – kissing and who-knows-what – that young Master Beornwulf, the Mercian Lord who comes here so often. We know why now!"

Æthelgifu felt her stomach twist and turn. Tears had to be quickly suppressed, and she struggled to resist striking out with her nails to do harm to her old friend. The word "Betrayer" filled her mind while she took deep breaths, but meantime Asser spoke.

"What were you thinking of, Sister? Have you and this young man some sort of relationship? Speak, now – or your abbess will have to punish you severely."

Tate found an inner strength. Lifting her head and commanding a voice that was almost defiant, she announced,

"Yes, indeed. I have heart-love for him and he for me. More than that, mind-love too!"

"But you have promised truth-love to your Lord God, have you not?" asked Asser, typically for him using clever word-play to make his point. "Such faithfulness, discipleship, can not be thrown aside, surely? And your vows to the abbey – obedience, stability?"

"I do not care. I renounce them all. Beornwulf and I plan to leave together — forever."

Æthelgifu had to sit down. The shock to her

emotions proved too strong. In a hoarse voice she whispered,

"You, you...traitor. Not only are you a traitor to me, to the abbey and the religious life here, but you are also a traitor to your country!"

Tate looked confused, so Æthelgifu went on quickly, with a louder voice. "Why do you think the All-powerful God allows the heathen Danes to destroy so much, to raid and kill? Think of Alwyn. Think of so many innocent Saxons slaughtered by these savages. Why? Because of our sins, the sins of the Saxon people, that's why! Why do you think my father founded this abbey and the one at Athelney and others?"

The tension in the room was palpable, as the abbess continued heatedly, answering her own question, her voice harsh and cutting as a sword blade.

"For us to pray to change God's mind, why else? To deliver us from the consequences of our sins. Just as in the Gospel of Luke, the widow pestered the judge until he changed his mind. That's what we're doing! We are like that widow-woman and God the judge. We exist to pray not only for the souls of our dead but for the total defeat of our country's enemies, the heathen Danes and all who invade countries to plunder and kill. We are warriors, Sister, no less than the soldiers next door. To leave our field of battle is ... is desertion!"

She sat back, exhausted and red faced, with eyes still blazing. Asser nodded, impressed both by her knowledge of Scripture and the strength of her loyalty to Wessex. A true daughter of a worthy king. The gentle monk approached the now distraught Tate, and spoke softly to her, taking her hands in his.

"Listen, daughter. If you leave here with Lord Beornwulf, to protect your honour, it will be said that he abducted you. Unfair on him, yes? Were you to have a child with him, and then, for whatever cause, Beornwulf dies, that son or daughter would not be allowed to inherit any of their father's property. Nor you, either. Your family would not take you back. You would be destitute. You'd likely starve. If the child were killed, for any reason, half the normal compensation would go to the father's family, but your half would go not to you, but to the king."

Tate looked up at the speaker, desperately taking in all the implications of what he was saying.

"This is law number eight in King Alfred's new set of laws. I helped him draft them, and it was to discourage foolish young women like yourself from contemplating doing what you have just expressed. So now, go and kneel at the feet of your abbess, and express true contrition for the alarm you have caused her. Mistress Edith, kindly go to the Guest House and tell Lord Beornwulf that he is no longer welcome here and to take his leave immediately."

After Tate made her grovelling apologies and tearful expressions of remorse, her abbess bid her to retire to the church and stay there in darkness, in cold, and without food all night. Tate did not delay, for being in the company of her erstwhile friend was too painful.

Æthelgifu, now calm, took the monk's hand in hers, and looking up into his eyes, appealed to him.

"I know, Brother Asser, that you are writing an account of my father's life. Please, please tell him nothing of this. Nor of another terrible secret."

She then confided in Asser the fact of the loss, by theft, of the Holy Cross relic. He swore on his word not ever to reveal a word of this — as it would bring no honour either to the abbey nor even to the king himself.

CHAPTER 10
LIFE SETTLES DOWN

AS THE FIRST WINTER DREW near, the larger storage buildings filled up with grain, racks of root vegetables and apples, and sacks of dried peas and beans. The harvest had been good and provision for the whole community over the freezing months was assured. Cats kept the mice and rats away from the grain, and several of the pigs were fattened up for slaughter. Cheeses made in the spring were brought out ready for the kitchen. This first winter was to be largely survivable.

The only problem was an outbreak of fevers which started in November and killed three of the Handmaids and two of the lay workers by Christmas. Three other women Religious died before Spring — two young novices and an elderly widow, along with four of the slaves, three male and one female. What killed them varied, from fevers, infected wounds and heart attacks for some of the women, to falling from scaffolding while building, being crushed by a falling piece of masonry and being trampled by a panicking cart horse for the male slaves.

One young Welsh girl slave almost died from poisoning when ingesting a herb she thought was medicinal, but was toxic. The two Infirmarian Handmaids, who were training her in the healing arts, chided her remorselessly when she recovered. Their patients, largely labourers and their wives of the burh or abbey-owned villages, did well, mostly responding to the poultices, infusions, cleansings and prayers of the Sisters. Some died despite the best of care. Æthelgifu, who had herself served an apprenticeship in the infirmary at Wimborne, took a particular interest in the work of the nursing Handmaids and their staff. The infirmarian monk from Muchelney Abbey, whose knowledge was widely celebrated throughout Wessex, was drafted in to introduce more efficient herbal and plant-oil remedies and precise surgical procedures, including amputations. The Infirmarian Handmaids were terrified at first of wielding a knife and saw, especially on patients who screamed throughout, but with guidance and reassurance they became skilful practitioners, saving the lives of many patients suffering from infected wounds or crushed bones.

As the winter months passed, the daily routine of prayer, work, eating and sleep, was enlivened little but by visitors, mainly monks invited to teach the Sisters new skills. With the departure of the Athelney monks, Pepin and Mark, others were called in to advise on copying manuscripts, from preparing calf-skins for parchments, to advanced calligraphy and creating intricate coloured drawings around certain initial letters. They demonstrated how to create inks from different coloured dyes and how to apply finely beaten gold leaf.

These tutors were invited from the abbeys nearby — such as Glastonbury, or even further away Malmesbury, reknowned for its scholarship. Some were sent from Winchester and brought with them news from the court, of which Æthelgifu never tired of hearing. Matteo, Asser's replacement as head instructor in Latin, remained as a popular figure, lodging with the mass-priest and helping out with this quiet man's growing family. There was no inclination to call on any monks from Athelney. Many of them there, all foreigners, had left due to bitter infighting and been replaced with secular clergy — many married or with concubines. During the occasional visits from Abbot John, usually on his way to the coast to receive some more monks from abroad, Æthelgifu contrived to be engaged elsewhere for as much of the time as possible. His departing figure always brought joy.

The children in the learning-house continued their lessons, apart from those periods of harvest when even the youngest ones were called to field-work. They were provided with chalk and slates and learnt to read and write in both Latin and their own language. For the older children and the Handmaids, King Alfred himself provided books from both Classical and Christian traditions in English translations from Latin so that the great knowledge from the past could be learned and passed on. If free from abbatial and liturgical matters Æthelgifu spent much time in the day reading and in the night recalling what she had read in order to commit it to memory.

Evenings in the Great Hall were the times everyone liked best. After the main meal was Recreation Time. Sitting at trestles on either side of the fire pit the women could chat or play board games — chess was popular. Sometimes young Hannah brought her harp and sang songs that she remembered or that she invented. The ones most requested were about the sweetness of homelife, when the harvest was gathered and fruit grew in abundance. Other traditional sagas told of seafaring and discovering new lands. Æthelgifu encouraged the singing of songs about stories from Scripture, or of saints who had done wonderful works. When it was the turn of timid Elswith, she refused, claiming to have no talent for singing, with a poor memory for words. Nor could she compose any songs, as so many of the others could.

"Come now, Elswith. Have you not read Bede's account of Caedmon in the time of Abbess Hild of Whitby? He used to leave the assembly rather than take his turn, until one night while he slept, he dreamed he was singing wonderfully, about God's creation. He repeated the song from his dream and, with Abbess Hild's encouragement became a monk and spent his time learning Scripture and turning it into song. So, maybe you should sleep on it, Elswith, and tomorrow find you have a golden tongue." Everyone laughed, including Elswith, and the evening continued in good humour.

On special feast days, other people, beside attendant servants, were allowed into the Great Hall: the priest and his wife, Matteo, Grimbald and any of the visiting monks. Then the harp would be passed from one singer to another so that those who could, entertained the others with songs. If a scop were staying in the burh, or accompanying a noble guest, he would be invited to recite a poem such as the Advent lyrics, or allegorical animal verses such as *The Phoenix, The Panther* or *The Whale*. Sometimes, for fun, the scop would recite a number of riddles, always popular if sometimes rather bawdy. If he was staying over several days, he may have enthralled his audience with epic verse such as *Beowulf* and seafaring sagas.

One festive evening, the Handmaids hosted several ealdormen, who were breaking their journey from Winchester to Devon, along with Cynehelm, the Shaftesbury thegn with his wife, and Chad, the reeve. The noblemen had their scop with them, brought along to entertain them with songs and stories on their journey.

After the scop had entertained the company with several short songs, he asked for requests. Sister Gifu spoke out, requesting her favourite poem, *The Dream of the Rood*. At once Aethelgifu looked over to Chad in alarm. The famous epic celebrated a dream about the Holy Cross. Just as she feared, at the conclusion of the celebrated poem, Cynehelm called out.

"My Lady Abbess, tell me, why is the relic that your father gave you not on display, the portion of the True Cross given him by a Pope?"

Other mutterings rose up, prompted by this recollection of the precious endowment. As Æthelgifu desperately thought of a response, Chad, whose drinking horn had just been filled up with mead by a servant, made to stand, but stumbled awkwardly drenching Cynehelm, his neighbour. With a loud shout of surprise, the warrior reared up from his bench, and trod on the hound lying under the table who yelped and set the other dogs barking. Chad and a servant set to wiping mead from the thegn's clothes amid much laughter from the assembled company.

Encouraged by Master Asser, Æthelgifu began the practice of reading aloud during meals, as was the tradition in many religious houses. The abbey's growing collection of books afforded this to be done. Works they owned included *Lives* of various saints, or Bede's historical works, and King Alfred's own translation of Beothius's *Consolation of Philosophy*. A secure wooden box with a strong iron lock was made for the abbey to keep their precious books safe. This book-hoard was among the most precious of the wealthy abbey's possessions.

CHAPTER 11
HORROR AND JUSTICE

THREE YEARS NOW PASSED SINCE Shaftesbury Abbey was founded and Æthelgifu installed. She was finding that decision-making came quite easily — she knew instinctively how to weigh up all sides of an issue in order to come to a conclusion. She was being acknowledged as an approachable yet fairly strict abbess, consistent and empathetic, one in whom her Sisters could have confidence. Those who initially begrudged her promotion as the King's daughter now accepted her worthiness in the exalted role of abbess.

She found she was no longer so intimidated by Prioress Edith. This latter acknowledged the undoubted abilities of her former protégée, and began to defer to her judgements. Edith herself proved a very capable administrator, working with Chad, of the abbey's large estate. The two of them would study the figures and balance the books, accumulating a comfortable surplus of money and goods to see the community through bad times. At one time they found that one of their tenants had not paid his tithe for two years, and so something needed to be done.

Chad summoned the churl and his titheman to come to explain his circumstances. Æthelgifu having been coached in her role by Chad, sat on her carved wooden chair of office before the High Table in the Great Hall. Chad and Prioress Edith stood either side. Servants stood in the shadows behind them, awaiting any instruction.

When the tenant farmer and his local leader arrived they apologetically gave all the reasons for the debt — his land being flooded after severe rainfall, ill health causing him to fall behind with tilling and planting, the death of his parents, wife and children to some disease, rats attacking his meagre stores.

"There's only one thing to be done," decided Chad after conferring with Æthelgifu and the prioress. "You will have to become enslaved — either that, or starve."

The man broke down, weeping, with his titheman comforting him as well as he could. Æthelgifu ordered some wine to be given to restore the man's equilibrium and a servant boy ran forward to obey. She then gave the two unhappy peasants some time to walk about outside, taking the air as a freeman for the last time.

"You can visit our church, and pray for your future," offered the abbess.

While they were temporarily gone, the heavy ornate chair was lifted down by servants from the platform on which stood the High Table. It was placed down on the floor alongside the firepit and opposite the main doors. The abbess, her prioress and her reeve discussed many matters of business until Edith was sent outside to fetch in the two peasants.

The prioress then led in the poor man, followed by his titheman, up to the abbess. The man, shaking with apprehension, knelt before her and lowered his head towards her lap. Following instructions whispered by Chad, she held the man's head in her hands and stated the terms of his enslavement — that he would offer loyal and obedient service to his Lady and her successors as abbess while he lived, that he would be hers to command in all things, and in return would receive her protection and sustenance. She released his head which he raised, smiling and relieved. It was a blow to the pride of a freeborn man, but a great comfort to know he would be provided for and saved from imminent starvation.

Æthelgifu was relieved that apart from that disturbing incident, all was running smoothly, and although the previous harvest was not so plentiful, the more lands acquired through donations made up for any shortfall. An unknown infection, the same that killed the new slave's family, and that did not respond to any herbal cure, did not leave the abbey community unscathed. Several of the older women succumbed, and even some of the youngest oblates. It seemed to cull the oldest and youngest, but left the middling age group untouched. The burial ground beside the stone church was beginning to fill up. Some babies of local churls, dying before being baptised, were buried where the thatched church roof dripped rainwater, in the belief that they would be 'sort of' baptised by that means eternally.

Then one day, horror was visited on the abbey.

Two of the gate-keeping guards, dragging a scruffy-looking churl between them, his clothes and skin impregnated with black grime, ran panting into the assembly yard which spread before the entrance to the Great Hall. All three shouted out in chaotic chorus, "Mother Abbess!", "Lady Prioress!" or, "Master Chad?", waving their arms to attract the attention of whichever notable was available to attend them.

As it happens, the three named authority-figures were conversing in the Hall with Cynehelm, the thegn of the burh. Interrupted and annoyed, all four appeared at the entrance, intent on discovering the cause of the racket. They descended the steps onto ground level and approached the guards and the peasant stranger. At the sight of them, the awestruck man cringed visibly, hugging his grubby hat to his chest and almost bowing to the ground. He uttered some inarticulate choking sounds.

"Well, come on, man. Out with it!" urged Chad, while Cynehelm drew his seax out of its scabbard to frighten the wight. Æthelgifu approached the man and laid her hand on his begrimed arm, saying gently, "Do not be afraid, good man. Say what it is you have come to tell us."

Thus encouraged, he began to speak, but his voice trembled and his tongue seemed to be stuck in his throat. She patted his arm and he looked at her face.

"Well, your holy ladyship, I shall tell ye, but please tell the master there to put up his great horrid seax, for it do frighted me terrible."

At a nod from the abbess, Cynehelm did as requested, but with a poor grace. He would have happily run the underling through for disturbing them, but he controlled himself. The man continued,

"Well, see, I was coming through the King's Forest, for I am a charcoal burner there, near the settlement of Gillingham, and in the autumn, I brings sacks of leaves to the burh here — for them to use for the animals to lie on. When I seed a sight most terrible. It would have fair made me sick up my food if I'd had any in my belly..."

"Yes, yes," barked Chad impatiently, "but what was that you found?"

"Well, good sirs and my ladies, it was a monk, sirs. A dead monk, one what had been dead overnight, methinks, for the wolves had got to it and ate off all his face and..."

Edith let out a cry of horror and disgust, "By all the Saints of Wessex, that's terrible indeed!"

Æthelgifu went pale but was composed enough to ask a question.

"You know that it, he I should say, was a monk, but could not tell who?"

"That's right, Mother. You be the Abbess, right? I come here and not to the burh 'cos I thought you could know who the dead monk was."

Cynehelm, as the senior soldier present, took control.

"Well, charcoal-burner, how do we know you didn't kill the good monk, to rob him, perhaps, and then thought you'd come here with your story rather than to the burh where we'd have given you swift justice?"

The two guards grasped the terrified man's arms, and following the direction of the thegn's pointing finger, began to march him, struggling and protesting, towards the burh.

"Do not harm him, Master Cynehelm, I beseech you," pleaded Æthelgifu, with Edith adding her voice to appeal for clemency. "It will go hard for any future wrongdoing to be reported if you punish the news-bringer."

"And all freemen deserve a trial," contributed Chad. "So until we learn more about this death, it's better to keep this woodman near at hand, but safe." He had to raise his voice as the thegn was striding away, and added, "Also, think too, all monks travel in pairs or groups, so he was likely with another at the time."

Cynehelm turned, "So it could have been an attack and the others fled? Animals, perhaps, or Danes – though I have not heard of any round here recently."

The thegn, anger abated, turned again to follow the guards and prisoner. He stopped and called back, over his shoulder,

"I'll get that peasant to show me where the body lies, and I'll send out parties to Athelney and other abbeys and priories to see if they're missing a Brother!"

Æthelgifu put her arm around a trembling prioress, and together they withdrew to the church to pray for the soul of the unfortunate monk. Chad went his way, lost in thought.

The next day brought the news that the monk was

indeed from Athelney, Master Mark — known to the Shaftesbury community from three years back. He had been travelling with Master Pepin to Shaftesbury, for some unexplained reason, when the pair were set upon by outlaws who, according to Pepin, stabbed Brother Mark and would have killed him too, if he had not outrun them. He had continued to run to Gillingham, lying hidden while recovering from the shock. It was there where Cynehelm's men found him, crouched behind the altar in the small church where the Abbey's mass-priest sometimes held Masses.

Brother Pepin was accompanied to Shaftesbury where he related the account of the assault. He then joined the covered corpse upon a cart which was given a military escort and was sent on to Athelney Abbey, where Abbot John would see that the deceased received decent burial. At the same time, Cynehelm set out with several warriors from the burh to track and, if possible, capture the outlaws. The thieves and murderers must have hidden themselves well in the woods, or ridden far away, for they were never caught. That put Cynehelm in such a bad temper that no one dared to cross him for days.

Some time later, on a clear sunny morning, Chad approached the abbess as she was walking with Tild. They were discussing the recent birth in the mass-priest's family, and hoping the infant would survive, unlike the previous baby. The two women looked up as Chad addressed Æthelgifu.

"My Lady Abbess, I watched how you treated that terrified woodman the other day. You got him to speak, where threats did not. So I think now the time is right for you to preside over our court. You have seen how things are done and justice served, now come, take up your rightful place as judge over cases committed on lands bestowed upon the abbey. We have a session this afternoon."

"Well, I, I ..."

"Of course, if you don"t feel you're up to it..."

Æthelgifu felt the knot in her stomach now rose to her throat. Her face reddened as she exclaimed, "Of course, if that is my duty, I shall be there, Master Chad."

Tild was left open-mouthed. "Well, my Lady, I've never known an abbess before, so did not know all that they had to do. My word, I couldn't do what you're doing — but you'll be fine, I'm sure."

Æthelgifu herself did not feel so sure, and left her young attendant in order to seek out Brother Grimbald.

He was in the building known as the Scriptorum where the parchment skins for manuscripts were stretched out over frames angled to catch the light. Mistress Cwenhild was in there hunched over a frame, ruling lines on one of the skins in preparation for inscribing text. The older monk was checking the straightness of the drawn lines, and stood up straight when the abbess entered.

"Greetings, Mother Abbess. What draws you here?"

When she explained what was to be asked of her, he went to find the scroll of the Charter issued by the king, her father, to the abbey on its inception. Opening a heavy wooden chest, he drew out a document embellished by a great red waxen seal, opened it and scanned the text.

"Well, my dear," he said, in an avuncular tone. Cwenhild looked up startled at the familiarity. He read out, paraphrasing,

"So, so, so... a hundred hides of land... yes, yes. Ah, here it is! I also grant the ruler of the abbey the right of soke — as you know, or are not sure, that means jurisdiction over a court for crimes committed on your lands... And then he lists here what category of crime — for *forsteal*, that is stealing or theft, and *hamsocne*, that is burglary or wrongful entry into a home, and *mundebreche*, or disturbing the peace. So there you are. You have the legal right to preside over the court, as Chad said. Of course, for a really serious crime, such as murder or treason for example, you could go to the the the *scirgemot*, the shire court, and ask the *scirereve*, or sherrif, to adjudicate, or even the king's own *witengemot* – but let's hope nothing of that kind will be needed here. I have attended other abbey courts, to offer advice and counsel, and shall do for you this afternoon, if you so wish. So do not be afraid. We will call on Holy Wisdom to inspire you, so go now and pray, my dear Abbess, as I shall too."

That afternoon Abbess Æthelgifu and Prioress Edith entered the Great Hall and seated themselves at the high table, Æthelgifu in the centre and the prioress a few seats away. The chairs on either side of the abbess were taken by Grimbald and Wilfric the mass-priest. The latter looked drawn and tired, having spent the previous night attending his wife after her painful labour, where it looked as though both she and the baby could die. The village midwife and Sister Infirmarian had done all they could, but now only time would tell if the two would survive. His wife urged Wilfric to fulfil his duty by attending court, while she would try to sleep. A visiting monk from Malmesbury, and Offa, a battle-scarred warrior and senior adviser to Cynewulf, the Shaftesbury thegn, were also seated at the High Table. As Æthelgifu sat down, Offa leaned over Grimbald,

"Lady Abbess do not be afraid to inflict as harsh a penalty as you like upon the miscreants here today," he announced with a self-satisfied smile. She nodded in acknowledgement, but he continued,

"For I have heard of another court where a young woman, no older than yourself, having her nose and lips cut off and then scalped, as punishment for cheating on her lawful husband."

"Heavens, how horrible!"

"Oh, don't worry about her, my Lady, for she died soon after. That's a real punishment, that is. Deters others who might be tempted."

Chad entered with two guards, one holding an accused man at the end of a rope binding his hands behind him. The churl looked pitiful, his head bowed and shoulders hunched. The three stood just to one side of the firepit, while Chad ushered into the back of the hall a whispering group of awed peasants and bid them be silent. He then walked around the firepit, to face both the dignitaries and the accused.

"My Lady Abbess and the noble Court of this Abbey of Shaftesbury, I present the case of this freeman, Leonfranc of Donheued, who has confessed to the stealing of a live hen from one Mistress Johanna, widow of Donheued. Because he has confessed – he had no choice as he was seen in the very act – this court is just called to pass sentence upon him. But before that, there are those present who wish to speak."

Offa, the thegn's rugged counsellor called out, "First, by your leave, my lady Abbess, I think we need to hear from the man himself. Speak, man, why did you do it, and why should you not hang for it?"

Leonfranc, a dishevelled man, barely out of his

teens, with a black eye and swollen lip, trembling, stuttered out quietly, addressing the ground,

"Please, Masters and Ladies, I am truly sorry for it, I really am." Encouraged to have spoken thus far, he continued more loudly looking up at his judges, "But my wife, you see, she is in child again — we have two bearns already, my Lords — and she is very sickly. As we had no good food in the house I thought an egg or two would be good for her, but when I approached the widow's hen to take the egg from under her, she did squawk so terrible that I just grabbed her and ran away into the woods, in a panic like."

Chad then asked, "So what became of the hen when you were caught?"

"Well, when the hue and cry went up, I just dropped it, from fear like, but I am afraid it got taken by a fox before it got back to the widow's house, where it roosts, inside, on her roof timbers, with the others."

Realising he was babbling, he stopped and resumed his study of the floor at his feet. Chad then called upon one of the peasants to approach. He shuffled forward, head bowed, holding tightly to his cloth hat in his hands.

"Please my Lords and Ladies, I am titheman of Leonfranc's tithe, and know him to be a good man, always willing to help others. With others he defended the village a month or so ago when it was attacked by a gang of Danes, and killed one of the heathens with his pichfork. So a good Christian Saxon man. He did not mean to harm the widow, as he knew she had many eggs, which she sold, along with her wool yarn that she spins. He would have repaid her for them, I have no doubt. Be merciful, please your lords and holy ladyships, as who will look after his wife and all his children if he is hanged or has his hands chopped off?"

The speaker, the leading man of the ten who made up the tithe to which Leonfranc belonged was then replaced by another villager, this time the victim herself.

"My lords and my Lady Abbess, I am a poor widow. My husband was killed by wolves in the forest ten years or more back, and my two sons in fighting the Danes. I live by scrapping — collecting scraps of wool from bushes and gorse — and spinning it into yarn. I also collect oak galls which I sell by the sack to the abbey of Wimborne, and soon I hope to sell to you here, as you'll be wanting them for making ink to do your holy writing. Do scratch the vellum beautiful it does. Other than that, I have a dozen hens and sell their eggs. This Leonfranc stole my Mildred and she got herself killed. But I don't want him to hang for that, all the same."

Then Æthelgifu spoke, addressing the guilty man.

"What do you do to live on, Leonfranc?"

"Well, my Lady Mother Abbess, I do have my bit of land for growing things, and my fifteen sheep I keep up on the hills, about to be sheared, they are. Other than that, just things I do in the village. And my wife, she spins, of course."

The judges then turned their heads to each other to discuss Leonfranc's fate.

"A hundred lashes," said the thegn's counsellor. "Plus, a fine equivalent to ten hens."

"Be just, but merciful," advised Grimbald, to which Wilfric nodded.

"A week in the stocks and branding," contributed the Malmesbury monk.

"It's up to you, my Lady Abbess," called out Chad from the floor. Æthelgifu paused, thinking, all eyes upon her.

She then looked straight ahead, towards the accused and in a firm voice, declared:

"Leonfranc, being guilty of stealing from a poor widow, hear what the court orders in sentence. We shall spare your life, and much flogging, but you will receive ten lashes, to be administered in a public place in your village, and you will donate one whole fleece from your flock to the widow you have wronged."

She felt her knees shaking beneath her tunic, but when she looked at Leonfranc's expression of grateful relief, and at the smiles on the faces of all the peasants, especially on that of the widow victim, Æthelgifu knew she had made the appropriate judgement. Her whole body warmed with a surge of pleasure as her muscles relaxed. Of the men beside her, apart from quiet mutterings, there was little reaction. The prioress, though, was beaming.

Chad cleared the hall of one group of peasants and brought in another. These were more affluent-looking than the previous set, better fed and clad. The miscreants here were the two sons of the tenant of a water mill with a large riverside plot of fields and woodland. The two boys, for they were no older than in their midteens, stood roped together, looking terrified. Their parents stood behind them, the mother weeping noisily.

The victim, standing across the firepit, next to Chad, glared at the boys. It transpired that he was a stonemason, and had been travelling by cart with his family to Shaftesbury to help in the building of the abbey cloister. His vehicle had been stuck on the bridge near the watermill, a packbridge which was in a poor state of repair, and he had called on the young men idling nearby for help. Instead, having become drunk on mead, despite it being before noon, the two youths proceeded to beat and punch the mason, to scatter his tools and frighten his wife and children. Their titheman arrested them and brought them to Chad, knowing all ten men of the tithe would be fined if the crime went unpunished. The mason had been in no mood to drop the charges, and, despite the mother's pleas for mercy, no one in court supported the boys.

Æthelgifu's judgement this time was more severe. The boys were to be held in stocks for two days and nights, to be forbidden strong drink for one year, fined sixpence to go to the mason — to his delight — and ordered to rebuild the faulty bridge and to keep it in good repair. The whole court was well satisfied, and Chad barely disguised his amazement at the young abbess's wisdom. A true daughter of her father, he thought.

CHAPTER 12
MYSTERIES SOLVED

THE FIRST ACT AFTER this court session where Æthelgifu triumphed was for her to announce to Prioress Edith that Sister Wulfthrith was no longer to be subprioress, but instead be assistant cellarer, responsible for buying provisions and seeing that the kitchens were always adequately supplied. She declared this with such an authoritative tone and look, that Edith could do nothing other than mutter, "Of course, Mother Abbess," and left to tell her protégée the unwelcome news.

The following day's chapter meeting had a more relaxed and light-hearted mood. Sisters came in smiling and laughed easily at amusing remarks. Several volunteered for duties beyond their normal remit, although those involved in the kitchen were strangely subdued. The previous assistant cellarer was promoted to guest mistress, a vacant position after Tatswith's scandalous behaviour, and also put in charge of the household workers, free and slave. She was delighted, as were the servants in the precinct.

The next summer passed with a reasonable harvest, despite plentiful rain showers. On a day in September, Æthelgifu bowed to pressure from the lay people in the abbey and the town. She sanctioned the rite of Ætherbot, or Field-Remedy. This would normally be an annual event, but Æthelgifu had strong misgivings about it and had not permitted it in previous years.

Before dawn, four churls who worked abbey-owned land, went down to a field on the south of the hill, and dug out four clods of earth, enough for each man to carry in two hands. They applied a poultice to the root base of each clod, made up of yeast, honey, milk and oil mixed in with aromatic herbs. Then they brought them up the slope and entered the church with them, where they were received by Wilfric who then blessed the clods.

After Mass, a small group of the lay women came forward carrying four small crosses, just inches high. These they stuck into the soil, one to each clod. Then the clods, still held by the four churls, were taken in procession — lay folk first, monastic women and the priest following — down the steep hill and back into the field. Just as dawn was breaking, one of the four men turned to face the sun, then turned fully around three times, holding aloft his clod, and calling out,

"Holy Guardian of the Heavenly Kingdom, come, fill the earth that the crops may grow and flourish!"

Then the sods were placed on the ground and a plough brought forward. The priest approached it with a jar of ointment with which he then anointed it. The smell of fennel and frankincense, mixed with salt and oil, reached the noses of all present. Then a voice rang out, joined by others,

"Sacred, sacred, sacred Mother of Earth".

An ox was brought to the plough and placed in the harness, all the while the chant continued. A ploughman then began the day's labour of ploughing the field, beginning by facing the east, while a remnant of the crowd stayed behind to continue the chant, the others returning to their lives upon the hilltop. Æthelgifu climbed up the hillside path behind her chattering Sisters. She said nothing, but prayed inwardly that she had done the right thing.

One morning, while the Handmaids were at their chapter meeting, Tilde and Skadi, her assistant, were in the abbess's house busily sewing. Tild was repairing the hem of one of her mistress's gowns, worn ragged on the rough cobbles and mud, while Skadi darned where the brooch holding the garment had torn the fabric. They chatted and laughed together, recalling snatches of some of the songs sung by the women in the weaving house as they worked the looms. They heard the clatter of hooves and men's shouts outside, but paid little attention as guests were frequent at the abbey, and rarely involved them — there were servants enough. It sounded as if there were two visitors, one using a peremptory tone as he ordered to be shown to the abbess's quarters. At this, the two girls, startled, looked at each other and then quickly hid away their material, the better to greet the guests.

"Quick, Skadi, go and fetch the abbess, or at least send word that she has a visitor. Don't enter the hall, just open the door and get someone's attention. I'll tidy up here and receive whoever this is, though I think I know."

As the Danish slave-girl ran off to do her bidding, she passed Abbot John from Athelney with Master Pepin behind him. They stood by to let her pass, and then entered the pit-house, a single room with shuttered windows and wooden planks laid over a shallow pit, with space in the middle for the fire. Simply furnished with two low beds, three chairs and a table, there were wooden chests and various jars and boxes arranged round the walls. Tild stood her ground as the two men faced her, although she wanted to run to escape them.

"Wine, Father Abbot, and Brother Pepin? Or

would you prefer mead? I'll just go to fetch some, please wait here..."

She made a step towards them, as they stood before the door. Then she froze. Their bearing and demeanour frightened her, and even more, the words of the abbot.

"You are going nowhere. Stay where you are. You are Tild, are you not, Abbess Æthelgifu's servant? You were betrothed to Alwyn, the son of Reeve Chad – yes? He was killed some time ago and buried here, I heard it said."

"Why, yes, sir," she affirmed, resenting the name of her beloved being uttered in such a supercilious manner.

"Listen, then. There is something you must do. Quickly now, before your mistress arrives. See here." He held out his hand for Pepin to place an object in it – one about a foot in length, covered in a fine silk cloth. He then unveiled the object – a highly decorated reliquary with glinting gold and luscious jewels. Tild gasped.

"The Holy Cross!" she exclaimed in wonder.

"Indeed, this is the one. Brother Pepin here, er, what shall I say, acquired it shortly after that fool Chad hid it away. Too good for a house for women – that's right, isn't it, Brother?"

"Yes, indeed. Why her father had to give such a treasure to her and not to us, an abbey for men...I couldn't stand for that. It should have been rightfully ours."

"Anyway, here it is now. This is what Master Mark was returning when he, unfortunately, met his end. This good brother here could not accept that it should be returned, so argued with Mark somewhere near here in the forest. The argument got a little out of hand... Anyway, I decided that it would be better to return it as we cannot risk exposing or selling it."

"So you killed Master Mark?" blurted out Tild, without thinking.

The abbot quickly approached her, drawing out a seax from his belt as he handed back the precious relic to Pepin. With his free hand he grabbed Tild's shoulder and brought the blade up to her throat. Her hands tried to pull at his wrist, but her strength was no match for his. Pepin stepped up to her and with his free hand, grabbed one of hers and held it down. Abbot John then brought his face close to Tild's and rasped out his terms.

"Listen, stupid girl, you have one chance or I'll kill you, if not now, then shortly. You are to say this to your mistress — Listen! Say that Alwyn took it, yes, your betrothed, and his brother Edwin found it after Alwyn died, hidden in his effects. When he came to us at Athelney accompanying Brother Mark's body, this Edwin tried to sell it to us. You tell her that. We took it in for safekeeping and now return it. The Feast of the Exaltation of the Cross will be celebrated soon, and we thought you should have it to display for that. Now you, you say all that, or else..."

"No, no, never. I could never say that about Alwyn, or Edwin. That's..."

"Silence, little fool. You have no choice."

"Yes, she does!" announced a determined voice behind them. Æthelgifu had heard what had transpired, having left the chapter meeting early with a headache. She had arrived very shortly after the men's entrance and had been listening beside the doorway. Skadi was with her and had also heard almost everything.

Abbot John turned in confusion, releasing his hold on Tild and returning his seax quickly to his belt. Pepin stood, mouth open, holding the reliquary with shaking hands. His fate could be decided instantly and it would not be pleasant.

"Skadi, fetch Master Chad and the priest. Tell no-one else. Quickly, girl."

She then turned to her bewildered-looking servant.

"Tild, you are to swear to tell no-one of what has happened here today. There are only four others who know about the fact the relic went missing, the two who are coming now, Brother Asser, and Prioress Edith." Tild nodded with greater exaggeration than strictly needed.

Abbot John felt weak, and sat down uninvited. He had not expected this young woman to be so in charge of her powers and authority. Pepin was almost fainting with consternation. Æthelgifu bid him sit too, before he fell. She wanted both men to be so detained. She then requested Tild to offer her guests some wine, which they gladly took and drained their goblets. She was elated — with the return of the relic the burden of worry and concern was lifted. The mystery had been solved and none of her own people or her friends was implicated — just that odious monk and his abbot from Athelney.

Chad and Wilfric, the mass-priest, arrived together, breathless from running. They looked amazed to see Æthelgifu holding the precious reliquary, standing guard over the two monks. She quickly explained all that she had learned from overhearing, sparing no detail of the threats to Tild. The expressions on Chad and the cleric turned to anger, and Chad drew his own seax and would have lunged at the men had not Æthelgifu held up the relic in front of him, causing him to freeze and then relax. She handed it to Wilfric, not before bestowing a kiss upon it.

"No, Master Chad, we must be circumspect in this matter. If it were known that we allowed the holy relic to be stolen from our safekeeping, we would incur the anger of my father and all our benefactors."

She turned to the monks, and continued, "And if these so-called holy men were known to steal, to conceal and to murder — not to mention threaten an innocent young woman in my employ — their lives would be ended in too ghastly a manner to contemplate. No, I declare that you, Brother Pepin, must go into permanent exile abroad. Go, and never be heard of again on these shores, or I will tell my father all. And you, Abbot John, for all your scholarship you have not yet learned how to be an honest, Christian man. You can return to Athelney and we shall say no more, relying on your own conscience to supply suitable penances. Your crime, remember, is far worse than our failing, so be sure we will report you if we hear of anything that slights the reputation of a religious house of Wessex."

All the men looked at this young woman in amazement and, in two cases, grudging admiration. In such a short time the young, tremulous teenaged nun had developed into a confident woman of authority. They saw in her the female image of her father Alfred — the great warrior, noble leader, devout Christian, cultured man of letters and pursuer of justice. Her older sister was to lead armies into battle. She, Æthelgifu, was to lead a flourishing community of women into becoming one of the greatest religious institutions in the land.

· · ·

WE DO NOT KNOW for how long Æthelgifu lived and ruled over the Abbey of St Mary and the Holy Cross (as it was called at that time), as her successors' names do not appear until that of Herelufu in 966. Her brother Edward succeeded their father as King of the West Saxons in 899, and his son Athelstan, building on the military successes of Æthelgifu's sister, Athelflad, Lady of the Mercians, united both Wessex and Mercia with Northumbria, becoming the first King of England. Shaftesbury Abbey continued to flourish, becoming one of the richest and most influential in the land. The Welsh monk Asser became Bishop of Sherborne in the 890s and wrote the 'Life of King Alfred' from which much of our knowledge of his reign derives.

GLOSSARY AND NOTES

Nuns were known as **Handmaids of the Lord**, *Ancillae Domini,* and in the ninth century were probably addressed as Mistress, or possibly Lady. Sister and Brother would be used only within the community, and Mother only for the Abbess. Priests and monks would probably be called by name or Master. Sources are largely silent before the tenth-century Benedictine reforms.

Society, in order of rank. **King**, elected by the **Witan**, or body of **ealdormen**, warrior-nobles, at their court, the **Witanagemot**. His **Lady** is not a crowned queen (since a previous queen poisoned her husband!). Their sons are **Athelings**, royal aspirants to the throne. **Thegns** are lords, landowners obliged to serve the king in battle. Titles and lands may be inherited or earned. Below them are **churls**, freeborn peasants with rights, such as attendance at courts, bearing arms; and duties, such as paying duties to the king or his lord, and serving in a **Fyrd**, or muster. The unit of land sufficient to support a churl's (extended) family was a **hide.** If killed, his family could exact 200 shillings in recompence. At the bottom rank are **slaves**, either captives in war (a humane alternative to mass slaughter), condemned to loss of liberty as punishment, or reduced to it by poverty.

The **Frankpledge** is an oath sworn by all free males from 12 to 60 committing themselves not to break the law, to report offences and to belong to a **tithing**, a local group of ten families. The head of a tithing, or responsible leader, was the **titheman.**
Franks belonged to either West Francia (later, France) or East Francia (later, Germany).

Child oblate, a child 'offered up' (from Latin, *oblates*) to God to be brought up in a religious house. Alfred allowed the adult oblate the right to choose to continue in religious life, or not.
Postulant is a candidate or probationer for a religious order. **Novice** is accepted into the order for a trial, learning period (in the **Novitiate**), until becoming

Fully Professed by taking life-long vows. In the Benedictine Order these are of Stability (to the house entered), Fidelity/Conversion to the monastic way of life (includes poverty and chastity), and Obedience (to Superiors as to God). The Founder, St Benedict of Nursia, Abbot of Monte Casino (480-550) wrote a **Rule** in 516 to govern life of religious in community. **Vowess** was a widow, who took vows, but who was not a virgin (a requirement of **Handmaids of the Lord**). An **Abbess** was not under obedience to a **Bishop**, but only to the **Pope** (and the King) — although this became a subject of dispute. A **See** is the territory of a bishop. Sherborne was a bishopric before becoming an abbey.

A **Lectern** is a reading stand, holding a **Sacramentary**, book containing text for church services, or **liturgies.** A **Lectionary** contains passages from Scripture for liturgies, and a **Psalter** is the complete set (150) of biblical Psalms. These are recited or sung during the **Offices,** or Liturgy of the Hours, the set times of prayer. These are **Matins** (2 a.m.), **Laud** (Dawn/5 a.m.), **Prime** (early morning/6 a.m.), **Terce** (mid morning/9 a.m.), **Sext** (noon), **None** (3p.m.), **Vespers** (6p.m.), **Compline** (before retiring). The **Triduum** consists of the three Holy Days from evening on Maunday Thursday, includes Good

Friday, and Easter Saturday's Midnight Mass, and concludes on Easter Sunday evening. A **mass-priest,** the *messe-preost*, conducted services of the Mass and sacraments, in private chapels for lords and his tenants, religious communities, or towns, but had no pastoral responsibilities. Alfred deplored the ignorance of many of these of the Latin words they used.

Goddess Frey is the goddess of fertility in Norse mythology, whose symbol is a boar.
Valhalla is the glorious home of warriors who die in battle, sword in hand, in Norse belief.
Nissers, in Norse folk-myth, are little old men, sometimes just inches tall, with short tempers, who demand gifts of tiny clothing and foodstuffs, or they can be dangerous.
Elves, however, are in Saxon pre-Christian folk-belief and are human-like but with semi divine/diabolical attributes, some shining bright, others hidden and dark. They can bring disease, aches and pains, and cause drownings and falls. Associated with trees, forests, rivers and hills, they can also blight harvests, curdle milk and be a general nuisance.
A **seax** is a single-bladed long knife used in combat.
A **Freemartin** is an infertile cow, born twinned with a male and with male characteristics.
Love, *lufu*, can be *heort-lufe*, heart-love; *mod-lufe,*

mind/heart love, or *treow-lufu*, faithful love — and many other compounds.

Notes

What we know from history:

- Aethelgifu was the third child and second daughter of Alfred and Ealhswith
- As a sickly child, Æthelgifu spent her childhood as an oblate in a religious community
- The hill-top burh of Shaftesbury was developed by Alfred around AD 880, after his impressive victory over the Danes at the battle of Edington
- Æthelgifu was brought to Shaftesbury around AD 888 to found the first abbey for women
- Alfred presented the abbey with a portion of the 'true/holy cross' previously given to him by Pope Miletus
- Aetheligifu led a community of noble Saxon women for a number of years.
- Abbot John, known as the 'Old Saxon' led the community of foreign monks at Athelney Abbey, which failed to flourish

- The monks Asser and Grimbald were drafted into Shaftesbury Abbey in its early days to help with its foundation
- Scenes here of abbey life, court cases, enslavement practices, and beliefs, both pagan and Christian, are imagined, although based on historic accounts

ABOUT THE AUTHOR

Deborah M Jones is a retired theologian, editor and writer. Now, among many other activities, she works as librarian at Shaftesbury Abbey, Dorset, helping to create a research centre for studies on religious life between Saxon and Tudor times. This book, the first of a series of fictionalised accounts of certain abbesses at Shaftesbury Abbey, helps to bring alive the women whose voices were not much heard, yet whose achievements were highly significant.

ALSO BY DEBORAH M JONES

Murder mysteries in the Julia Deane series:

The World according to Julia

Julia's World goes West

Julia's World in Tune

The Battles in Julia's World

(In preparation) Julia's World: All at Sea.

Nonfiction

The School of Compassion: a Roman Catholic theology of animals

For more information about Deborah and her books, visit www.deborahmjones.co.uk

Printed in Great Britain
by Amazon